Karl peeped out of his office, and his heart did a quantum leap.

"Jessica! Is something wrong?" He was beside her instantly.

She was holding a hanky to her face. He caught the word "...hurts."

"Your tooth hurts?" Karl's heart contracted. He couldn't bear to see her in pain. "There's nothing to be afraid of, Jessica," he said gently. Just looking at her filled the emptiness inside him, made him feel wonderful. "How long have you had this pain?"

She removed the hanky. Karl noted with relief that her face wasn't swollen. "Since the first of February."

"That long? And you didn't tell me about it?" It could be any number of things. "Where does it hurt?"

She put both hands above her left breast. "Here!"

Karl frowned. "There?"

Jessica nodded mournfully. "Remember the day at the mall?" As if he could forget. "That's when it all began. I believe it's caused by loving someone and not being sure if that love is returned."

Dear Reader,

Welcome to Silhouette Romance—experience the magic of the wonderful world where two people fall in love. Meet heroines who will make you cheer for their happiness, and heroes (be they the boys next door or handsome, mysterious strangers) who will win your heart. Silhouette Romances reflect the magic of love—sweeping you away with books that will make you laugh and cry, heartwarming, poignant stories that will move you time and time again.

In the next few months, we're publishing romances by many of your all-time favorite authors such as Diana Palmer, Brittany Young, Annette Broadrick and many others. Your response to these and other authors in Silhouette Romance has served as a touchstone for us, and we're pleased to bring you more books with Silhouette's distinctive medley of charm, wit and—above all—*romance*.

During 1991, we have many special events planned. Don't miss our WRITTEN IN THE STARS series. Each month in 1991, we're proud to present readers with a book that focuses on the hero—and his astrological sign.

I hope you'll enjoy this book and all of the stories to come. Come home to romance—Silhouette Romance—for always!

Sincerely,

Tara Gavin
Senior Editor

GEETA KINGSLEY

Project
Valentine

Silhouette *Romance*

Published by Silhouette Books New York

America's Publisher of Contemporary Romance

To my daughter—
whose beauty is "soul deep."

SILHOUETTE BOOKS
300 E. 42nd St., New York, N.Y. 10017

PROJECT VALENTINE

ISBN: 0-373-08775-6

First Silhouette Books printing February 1991

Printed in the U.S.A.

GEETA KINGSLEY

feels one doesn't have to be perfect at things to enjoy doing them. Singing (off-key), art (dot-to-dot pictures), homemaking (it takes real willpower to ignore dirty dishes and dust) and gardening (watching things grow) are all on her love-to-do list.

Her gypsy karma has led to travel all over the world. Home, at present, is California, where she lives with her husband and teenage son and daughter. Reading and writing stories have always been an important part of her life. A former elementary school teacher, her job title these days is professional dreamer.

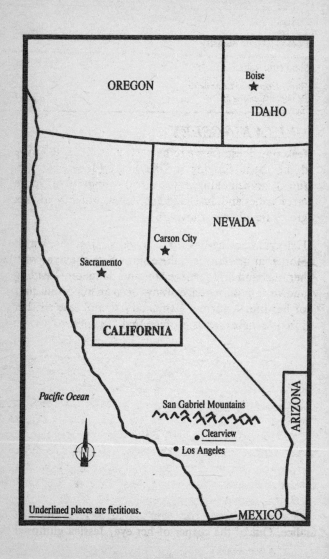

OREGON

Boise
★

IDAHO

NEVADA

Carson City
★

Sacramento
★

CALIFORNIA

Pacific Ocean

San Gabriel Mountains

ᗰᗰᗰᗰᗰᗰ

● Clearview
● Los Angeles

ARIZONA

Underlined places are fictitious.

MEXICO

Chapter One

Cold water arced from the fountain, hitting the parched spot at the back of Jessica's throat with gratifying precision. She closed her eyes and drank deeply. Water always quenched her thirst as nothing else could. Finding this water fountain had taken a while. Clearview Plaza was one of Los Angeles County's most modern, elegant shopping malls. Water gurgled out of elaborate fountains, rippled by in colossal artificial lotus ponds, but this seemed to be the only spot on the lower level where one could drink it.

Jessica took another big gulp, wishing it would change into some magic elixir and enhance her powers of persuasion. Talking, smiling and convincing people that a dog would fit nicely into their southern California life-styles was hard work. No one else seemed to have the ability to fall in love at first sight with the Great Dane as she had, and Arthur had to be adopted today.

The sudden snigger from behind her held no humor. Only malice. Out of the corner of her eye, Jessica glimpsed the pair standing behind her. It was eight months away from Halloween, so their outfits had to be normal, everyday wear for them.

Black. Metal. Leather.

The stiffening hair on the nape of her neck, the churning of her stomach, christened the duo trouble. Trouble looking for her. The fountain was set in a little alcove. The miscreants blocked her from passersby. No one knew she was here . . . or that she might need help.

Jessica let the water flow over her closed lips, pretending she hadn't noticed anything unusual, pretending she was still drinking. She had to buy herself some extra time.

It wasn't the first occasion she'd been mistaken for young and helpless. Under one hundred pounds, five feet tall, dressed casually, Jessica couldn't remember the number of times she'd been told she passed for a teenager. Fair game for this obnoxious pair.

Slowly, reluctantly, she straightened. Sometimes the best way to face a confrontation was head-on.

"Oops." The slight shove was a herald. There was definitely more to come.

Turning to face the young men, she gave them her I'm-one-tough-cookie look. "Excuse me," she said coldly.

Obviously unaffected by her glare, neither budged an inch.

"Sorry," snickered one, "he pushed me."

"So sorry," mimicked the other, stepping forward.

A sliver of fear replaced toughness. Jessica took a step back. The edge of the fountain dug into her back; the pair hovered over her like giant birds of prey. She was in a trap.

The water in her stomach had frozen to a block of ice, but her mind churned rapidly. Only rabbits froze in the face of danger. And look what happened to them. Clutching her bag, Jessica considered her options. Her wolf whistle would attract too much attention. She didn't want to risk attracting adverse publicity. Using a karate chop would mean having to file a police report. Staying here was the pits, though. She wasn't in the mood for kiss-and-tease with two juvenile Draculas. Maybe she could talk her way out. Jessica took a deep breath.

"What's your name, babe?" one of them asked.

The look in their eyes frightened her. She couldn't appeal to emptiness.

"Cat got your tongue?" They loomed closer.

Jessica put both hands up. As a barricade, a bar of melted chocolate would have been more effective.

"Let's see if we can't cure the dumb," the first one drawled, enjoying every moment of his self-assigned role of tease.

Every muscle in her body tense, Jessica waited for their next move. Hers would have to be karate. She wished she knew what came first. The blow or the yell. Television always made everything look too easy. The program she'd followed on self-defense had never explained what to do if a move didn't work. On the show everyone had fallen exactly where they were supposed to.

The pair closed in on her. Jessica opened her mouth and lifted her hands. When in doubt, she decided, do everything at once.

They were ripped apart like a sheet of paper. In the gap stood a man whose bulging biceps and the corded muscles in his neck were the only signs of strain as he effortlessly held the two struggling youths by the scruffs of their necks.

Jessica blinked. Then she quickly closed her mouth and let her hands drop to her sides.

"Are they bothering you?"

The query accompanied a laser-beam look that pierced right through her as her rescuer examined her from head to toe. Jessica felt he saw both what was on the surface and what was under it with that glance. Anger painted his features with tight, dark lines. No avenging angel could have looked more forbidding. Thank goodness he was on her side.

"We were just waiting for a drink," whined one of the pair.

"We didn't mean no harm," echoed his spineless counterpart.

The shake they received warned that the man was allergic to explanations.

"Are you all right?" Again that look. Roving, searching, *penetrating*.

"I'm fine." She pushed her glasses up nervously.

It was like watching two separate acts of a play at the same time. The first involved this man and the hooligans. Jessica could sense his anger, his intolerance of the game they had been playing. The second was solely between her and him. His expression offered her protection, caring, consideration. His manner told her she had nothing to be afraid of.

As rescues went, this was one of the best.

Why on earth hadn't she worn something else instead of the madras yellow pants and tank top covered with a loose red shirt? Her pink suit, the single strand of pearls, would have been so much nicer.

"Please let them go. I really am all right," Jessica said. Passersby were beginning to stare at them.

Giving the youths another shake, he allowed their feet to touch the ground. "Five minutes to get out of the mall," he gritted, "and then I'll give security a description of you two and file a complaint. The reason I'm letting you go is I think this is the first time you've pulled something like this. Am I right?"

Shamefacedly the youths nodded.

"Don't you have anything better to do with your time? Juvenile detention hall isn't any fun, believe me. Not to mention what it'll do to your futures to have police records."

He had their attention now. They both wilted, their heads hanging like top-heavy flowers.

Her rescuer wasn't impressed. "If you ever pull anything like this again, I'll personally see you are taken in. Now, apologize."

"Sorry," mumbled one late hero.

"Didn't mean to scare you," whispered the other.

Paper dragons. That's all they were. They vanished without a backward look.

Jessica was still trying to figure out how size could have so much power when she felt the arm around her shoulders. Startled, she looked up at the man beside her. A jolt went through her as their gazes collided.

"Let's go sit down." His voice had switched from dynamite tension to velvet concern. "They're only two kids bored out of their heads. Are you sure you're all right?"

Jessica nodded weakly. He was doing more damage to her composure than the two boys had. Tucking her into his side, his warmth wrapping her like a down comforter, he led her to a convenient wooden bench and made her sit.

It was a very long while since someone had made her feel so...so special. Jessica was glad she hadn't used her wolf whistle. His way was much better.

"Lean back and close your eyes," he commanded softly. "You look awfully flushed."

She did as he asked. Only because contact with his body had overheated her brain. Her glasses were slipped off her nose, and a large hand pressed against her cheek.

"Your face feels very warm. Take it easy. I'll be right back." The voice reminded Jessica of an echo in a cave. Resonant, deep, musical. With a timbre that lingered in the reaches of her brain.

"Count and breathe," she told herself sternly. "One and two and three and four. In and out and in and out. You've got to regain control before he comes back."

Jessica tried painting calm pictures in her mind. Blue skies, a field of flowers, a baby at its mother's breast.

She wasn't entirely successful.

Flashes from a pair of Rocky Mountain eyes, set in a craggy face, kept interrupting her visualization. Their color haunted her. They weren't the light brown of the lower slopes. More the dark brown of the peaks and the precipices. The power of his gaze was different from any man's. Jessica had never met anyone who made her feel so... so much a woman.

"Here, try this. It'll help combat shock."

Jessica's eyes flew open. He held out a disposable paper cup brimming full of juice. She took the cup from him with a hand that shook.

"It's fruit juice... the natural sugar will do you good."

Jessica blinked. Could juice douse the flames leaping up inside her? Heat had shut off thought, left room only for feelings. She should be running. Hard and as far away as she could get. Leaning back against the bench, Jessica sipped her drink slowly. One didn't hurry a dream along.

The man sat down beside her. "By the way, my name is Wagner. Karl Wagner."

"Jessica Hansen," she supplied in a croak.

"Are your parents here in the mall with you? Can I have them paged? Or are you here with a friend?"

He thinks I'm a kid.

That explained the *uncle-home-for-Christmas* voice. Acute disappointment cut away the rosy haze with a machetelike stroke.

Jessica got to her feet. "I'm here by myself." If one didn't count the officials, the volunteers, the twenty-odd animals from the Los Angeles County Humane Society, that is. The badge pinned on her chest that read Project Valentine apparently didn't mean a thing to him. She ought to have made herself another badge. One that read Twenty-Three Going on Twenty-Four. Maybe then things would have been different.

A frown spliced Karl Wagner's wide brow. Evidently he didn't like the idea of her being here alone. Jessica frowned back. When would people stop equating petite with helpless? She wasn't about to let this man take over where her family had reluctantly left off. Rescuing her was one thing. Taking charge of the rest of her life was too much.

"If you'll wait a moment, I'll see you into a cab." Apparently he was oblivious to frowns. "I'm waiting for someone. That's how I noticed you at the fountain. As soon as those two boys appeared, I could smell trouble. Are you sure they didn't hurt you?"

His gaze skimmed her again from head to toe. Jessica's hand trembled as she straightened the shoulder strap of her bag. Of course he was waiting for someone. Men like him didn't hang around malls guarding secluded water fountains for amusement.

"I'm fine. Thank you for helping me." Jessica held her hand out.

Surprise flashed in his eyes as he took her hand and shook it.

Now, thought Jessica, *now*. This is where he looks into my eyes and sees I'm a woman.

It wasn't her day for telepathy. His expression didn't change.

"Let me give you back your glasses." He fixed them on the edge of her nose. "If you're sure..."

"I'm back!" The interruption was blond, already shoulderhigh to Jessica and anywhere between eight and ten years old. "I've got my cone and my presents. Promise you won't look at them?"

"This is Molly." Karl Wagner smiled at the girl as he introduced her to Jessica.

"Hi!" Over the ice-cream cone Molly treated her to a shy grin and a frank appraisal. Her warm, keen, curious eyes riveted Jessica. Rocky Mountain eyes.

"Hello, Molly!"

His daughter. It made perfect sense. Caring came naturally to a parent. It explained his protectiveness, too. Jessica's overactive imagination supplied a picture of a green-eyed blonde to go with the pair in front of her. Someone Junoesque. And beautiful.

She swallowed the boulder in her throat. Didn't he know only single knights could rescue maidens in distress and steal their hearts? Oh, well. Time to get on with her life. Time to let Karl Wagner get on with his.

Before she could get the right words out, he turned his head and said, "Excuse me. I'll be right back."

Jessica looked at his broad back as he walked up to a security guard and stopped him. Obviously the five minutes he'd given the troublemakers were up. Taking in his designer jeans and the soft gray shirt, the black leather running shoes, Jessica curled her toes inside her sneakers.

"Married," she muttered to herself. *"Taken. Out of bounds. Not available."*

Her mind refused to accept it.

Jessica looked at Karl Wagner again. It was amazing, the way he'd appeared out of nowhere when she'd needed help. What was even more amazing was the fact that though she always insisted on absolute independence, she'd enjoyed every moment of her rescue.

"Oh!" The squeak and the ice-cold feeling on her foot accompanied the sighting of its cause.

Jessica's left sneaker supported the double scoop of strawberry ice-cream that had so lately been in Molly's cone. The girl stared in dismay at the tilted cone in her hands. Fear held center stage on her face as she looked at Jessica. Tears waited in the wings. Molly stammered, "I'm sorry. I . . . It just happened by itself."

"Don't worry," Jessica reassured instantly. She had a lifetime of experience with things that happened by themselves. "I can clean it up."

There was a slight problem. If she tried walking, the scoop was going to slide off her shoe and make a bigger mess on the floor of the shopping mall. She looked around for something to remove it with.

"Molly, let's go . . ." Karl Wagner's voice trailed away as his glance raced from Molly's empty cone to Jessica's foot.

Jessica barely opened her mouth before he swung into action. Taking the napkin out of Molly's hand, he lifted the ice cream off Jessica's shoe, disposing of it in a nearby dustbin. Pulling a large, man-size handkerchief from his pocket, he wet it at the fountain and then went down on his knees, scrubbing at the stain on her shoe.

"Stand still." The order came on the heels of her attempt to move her foot away. The words to say that she could take it from here died on her lips as one large hand cupped her calf to ensure she didn't move again.

The point of contact transmitted strange impulses to Jessica's brain. Her calf was really compacted oatmeal. Strange quivers radiated from her foot to the rest of her body, making her feel like a volcano about to erupt.

She wasn't used to men kneeling in front of her. Or cleaning her shoe. Her stampeding senses made her feel faint.

Get a grip on yourself. You're a twenty-three-year-old woman, not some heroine in a Gothic romance.

Modern men hated helpless females. And so far she'd been nothing else. Digging deep down for her Patton-tank look, Jessica fixed it on her face.

"I can do that." Unfortunately her voice didn't match her expression. Melted marshmallow was firmer. Karl Wagner kept on scrubbing as if she hadn't spoken. Molly stood by, watching the procedure.

As he knelt, the top of his head almost reached her chest. Jessica looked down at his thick, curly, black hair that invited touching. Invited rumpling.

She blinked as he looked up. His gaze slammed into her at sixty miles per hour. Every single thought in her head was exposed to it.

"Is your foot sticky?"

A picture of her shoe being removed, her foot being cleaned by those powerful hands, caused ten-foot-high waves in her imagination. Storm strength.

"No. It's not."

Pressing her foot to the floor, Jessica put all her weight on it. Not that she could stop a man who could lift two youths as if they were ten-pound bags of Idaho potatoes.

"There you go." He stood and looked at her. "Does that look all right?"

"That's fine," she mumbled. Who cared about the silly stain, anyway? She watched as he threw his handkerchief into the trash can.

"Molly and I would like to buy you a pair of sneakers to replace the ones you have on." His arm around his daughter's shoulders told the child that accidents happen to everyone. He didn't blame her for this one.

Jessica blinked again. "They're machine washable." At five dollars a pair, they were also expendable. Unlike the fine monogrammed handkerchief he'd just thrown away.

"I'm sorry I dropped my ice cream on your shoe." Molly meant every word of the apology.

Consideration and caring wasn't something this man would ever have to teach his family. They would grow up making it an integral part of their lives . . . just as he did.

Jessica smiled at the girl. "That's perfectly all right," she said gently. Extending the smile in the direction of the man's chin, she added, "Thank you for cleaning my shoe and coming to my rescue."

As she walked away, Jessica wondered why she'd avoided one last look at the Rocky Mountain eyes.

"Uncle Karl, we'll be late for the movie." Molly tugged at her uncle's sleeve. Why on earth was he standing still as a statue? She looked in the direction Jessica had taken. "What did that lady mean about you rescuing her? Was she in trouble?"

Karl Wagner stared down at his niece. "She's only about sixteen," he said gently. It was strange that Molly, who was so perceptive, should mistake Jessica Hansen for an adult. "And, yes, someone was bothering her."

Molly's mind was on the film they were to see. It promised to be bloody, scary and incredible. All an eight year old could ask for.

It wasn't till the part where the dinosaur swallowed the Empire State Building that she remembered something. Uncle Karl was funny. He'd said that Jessica was sixteen, but she wasn't. She was a grown-up. Couldn't Uncle Karl tell?

Project Valentine.

Fixing her mind on why she was here today, Jessica decided, might help coax it back to its normal even keel.

It had all started four weeks ago. The article in a Sunday edition of the *Los Angeles Times* had caught Jessica's eye. In an effort to find new homes for some of their abandoned animals, the Humane Society had come up with a novel plan. The animals would be on show in Clearview Plaza, a popular shopping mall in the city of Clearview, part of Los Angeles County, two weeks before Valentine's Day. Volunteers were needed to work with the animals on a one-on-one basis in the mall. What was expected of them wasn't difficult. Show the animals, share the background knowledge that was available and try to match prospective owners with the right pet. Officers from the Humane Society would be in charge overall, but the volunteers would do the actual "selling." Jessica's decision had been made by the time she'd finished reading the article. Ten minutes later she was at the Humane Society. And now, looking at Arthur, she remembered the first time she'd seen him.

The enclosure was barely big enough for the Great Dane lying in it. Tawny with a black face, he had a white patch on his chest. His lack of interest in her didn't surprise Jessica. He'd been through too much lately to trust another human quickly.

The expression in his eyes tugged at Jessica's heart. Anguish over being deserted by his owners lurked there, mingling with sadness that a lifetime of love and devotion had been rewarded with abandonment. It all added up to raw pain.

And it was up to her to do something about it.

"Why did they leave him? He's beautiful."

The officer who was showing her around said, "It isn't easy to take a dog along when moving, especially one as big as this. There could be other reasons. See that white mark on his chest?" Jessica nodded. "Well, that's not desirable in a purebred, fawn Dane. It's like a disqualification in a dog show and lessens his value."

His owners had left him just because he had a mark on his chest? The other reason made her sick. It hadn't been convenient to take him along. She wondered if anyone had loved the Great Dane or if he had just been another status symbol in a world of people who devoted their time to impressing others. The lump of anger in her throat made Jessica blink. Rage always produced tears. Crying wouldn't help anyone.

She took a deep breath. "I want to show this dog at the mall."

"What's the use of backing a lame horse at the races?" José Garcia asked reasonably, hitching his pants up over a belly that stretched the buttons of his shirt to popping point. "I like this dog, too, but that doesn't change the facts. Very few people want an animal this size. The odds are against him. Showing him would be a waste of your time."

I know best. A little thing like you should listen to me. It was all there in his voice, in his manner. The indulgence, the condescension. To Jessica it was like a red flag to a bull.

Eyes narrowed, she fairly spit her next words out. "When I called the Humane Society regarding Project Valentine, I was assured I could pick the animal I wanted to show, providing the animal would make a good prospective pet. Is this dog vicious?"

"No."

"Sickly?"

"No."

"Too old?"

"No."

The matter, as far as Jessica was concerned, was settled. Closing the distance between them, she tilted her head and gave José Garcia her fight-unto-death look. "Then I'm going to show him. He has as much right to another chance as any other dog in this shelter."

The officer looked at her face, seemed to make a snap judgment about indomitable fighters and sighed. With an expression on his face that would have made Job appear cheerful, he said, "Let's go into the office and take care of the details. You can show him, but don't blame *me* if no one wants him."

Jessica's mind snapped back to the present, to survey the scene in front of her. A central area on the lower floor of the mall had been roped off. The volunteers, each with an animal on a leash, formed an oval, facing outward. In the middle a folding table held all the necessary paperwork for releasing the pets to their new owners. Officials in blue and gray made sure everything was under control, talked to the public and spelled volunteers for breaks.

The Project Valentine banner attracted a great deal of attention with its heart-shaped pink and white balloons. The theme, Take Home A Real Sweetheart For Valentine's Day, had worked wonders so far. Fifteen dogs and three cats had already found homes.

But not Arthur.

Something about his look of patient suffering wrapped in regality had inspired the name on Jessica's third visit to the shelter. By then he'd begun to know her and greet her by wagging his tail.

"I'm back," Jessica announced, repinning her name tag under the Project Valentine badge. A quick glance at her watch revealed her adventures hadn't exceeded the thirty-minute break she'd been allotted. "Anyone stop by?"

José Garcia looked at her cautiously as he handed her Arthur's leash. "No one."

One long moment passed before she lifted her head and looked at him. On a scale of one to ten her smile would barely get a one for joy. For bravery it merited a twelve.

"Well, it's still early," she said. "Thanks for spelling me, José."

After he left, her imagination opened the door, let the doubts pour in. What if he'd been right all along? If no one adopted Arthur today? The next instant Jessica told herself not to be negative. The right person hadn't come along yet. When that person did appear, it would be a case of love-at-first-sight and happily-ever-after for Arthur.

She had to hold on to that thought.

There was a pattern to the day that kept repeating itself with frightening monotony. People looked at Arthur in wonder, stopped to find out what he ate, how much he weighed, if they could touch him. No one evinced the slightest interest in taking him home.

By two o'clock Jessica's face ached with the effort to keep a smile pinned on. Her heart ached with the weight of presentiment.

The odds are against him. Recalling the remark fanned the coals of her determination.

"I don't care how much experience José Garcia has, he has no right to make that remark about you," Jessica told the Great Dane rebelliously. "I know all about odds. I've faced them all my life. Impossible is just a state of mind. We'll find you a home yet."

A couple stopped, looked at Arthur and then moved on to the next dog without saying a word. Leash looped around her wrist, Jessica patted Arthur. Squeals of joy pierced the air as a little girl and her brother exclaimed over a terrier mix. The happy, newly adopted dog licked their faces in reciprocal joy. Jessica's throat tightened. She wanted a wedge of the same kind of happiness for Arthur.

"Success lies in fighting for what one believes in, not letting someone else tell you what you can and can't do." Lifting her right foot, Jessica rubbed it against the calf of her left leg to ease the cramp there. "I'm going to prove it by finding you a new owner today, a *better* owner." Her soliloquy tapered off as a couple stopped in front of them.

"What breed is he?"

"Great Dane."

"Bet he weighs a ton." They tittered, pleased by their own wit and slunk off with their arms twined around each other like bean runners needing support.

Beside her, Arthur lifted his head, stared at another dog nearby and then settled down again. Throat tight, Jessica looked at her watch. Three o'clock.

What if José Garcia was right? What if no one came by for Arthur in the next two hours? What if . . . ?

Jessica clamped down on her imagination. No, that wasn't going to happen. As long as she thought strong, she couldn't fail. Arthur would find a home by tonight.

"If I could have you, I would," she told Arthur for the umpteenth time. "But they are very strict about their no-pets policy in the apartment. If only there was some way I could afford a house . . ."

That wasn't possible on a computer programmer's salary. Not while she helped out her brother David whenever his funds ran low. Jessica searched her memory bank for anyone she knew who would fit the bill.

Worry checked all the bases she'd covered so far. Her lunch hour the past week had been spent talking about Arthur to anyone at work willing to listen. She'd put up huge notices by the coffee machine on each floor. Staying late one evening, she'd printed some flyers and paid the newspaper boy to place it on car windshields around the neighborhood.

The response had been disappointing. No one wanted a dog the size of Arthur. Besides, most people assumed it cost an arm and a leg to feed a Great Dane. Most people were right. But that wasn't the real problem. Finding a person who liked Arthur was. If only someone showed a real interest in the Great Dane, she was even willing to pay for part of his upkeep.

Restlessly Jessica's gaze roamed the mall. So many people, so little time.

The red dot she'd seen next to Arthur's name on José Garcia's pad this morning had scared her. Skewering the officer with her fiercest look, she'd demanded, "What's that for?"

"The shelter can only keep the animals for so long, Jessica," he'd replied gently. "Arthur's time with us is almost up."

Jessica closed her eyes briefly. The sands of time dragged her hopes along as they ran out on Arthur's life. Harsh reality waited impatiently to force its way in.

"Please," whispered Jessica. There had to be a patron saint of dogs somewhere, with more than human powers. "*Please.* We need a miracle."

Two minutes later Molly and her father crossed Jessica's line of vision and halted in front of the bookstore. Jessica stiffened as neon bulbs came on in her head.

Strong. Caring. *Perfect.*

Molly looked over at their group. Interest flickered in her face as she saw the Project Valentine sign. Her eyes opened wide as she noticed Arthur. A flash of recognition lit her face as she saw Jessica. She tugged at her father's hand, said something. The pair walked over.

Jessica fixed a smile on her face. Out of the corner of her mouth she said, "This could be our big break, Arthur."

The man looked from her to the badge that bore her name and nodded briefly. Their earlier encounter might never have been.

Not that there was much to hold his gaze, Jessica acknowledged humorously. Her straight, chin-length, toffee-colored hair and eyes to match weren't exactly spectacular. Her mouth was too full, the rest of her features just there. She pushed her glasses up.

"Hi!" greeted Molly with an infectious grin.

"Hello again." Dropping ice-cream on someone's foot forged an instant bond. They smiled at each other like conspirators. Jessica kept her eyes on the girl while every nerve ending informed her exactly where Karl Wagner was.

"Is he yours?"

Jessica looked from Molly to the dog in momentary surprise. For a couple of heartbeats she'd forgotten Arthur. "No, he belongs to the Humane Society of Clearview."

"Did you bring him here so people could learn about Great Danes?"

"No." Jessica swallowed hard, forcing herself to concentrate. Odd little quivers kept interrupting her thinking. "We brought the dogs to the mall today hoping to find good homes for them."

"What's his name?" Molly asked.

"We don't know. The Humane Society found him wandering the streets."

The blond head bobbed wisely. "My teacher told us all about the Humane Society. They round up strays and take in dogs no one wants. Did his owners just leave him, do you think?"

"That's most probably what happened."

Karl had apparently just come along so his daughter could satisfy her interest in the dogs. His eyes already held a trace of impatience as he looked over the other dogs. There was no real interest there. Jessica's heart sank.

The girl put a hand out to the dog.

"Don't touch him, Molly," Karl Wagner snapped.

"Arthur wouldn't hurt a soul," Jessica interposed quickly. "He's wonderful with children. I had a little girl here earlier who stepped on his paw by mistake, and he didn't turn a hair. Good nature is a primary characteristic of Great Danes."

"Arthur?" The deep voice pounced. "I thought you said he didn't have a name?"

Jessica felt the color ride up under her skin. She blinked rapidly. "It's my own private name for him."

Defiantly she met his gaze. That look of his was really something. She had a feeling the contents of her brain were on view.

Molly put out her hand and let Arthur sniff at her. Then, at Jessica's nod, she touched Arthur's head.

"Great Dane?"

"Purebred." The squeaky pitch of her voice was humiliating. Disgusted by the fact that her sales pitch was so hard to find, Jessica took a deep breath and tried again. "They make excellent companions and great watchdogs. I don't know why anyone would install an alarm system when they could have a dog instead. Research has proved pets provide excellent therapy. They improve heart function, lower blood pressure, ease anxiety." A quick breath, and Jessica rushed on. "They are definitely man's best friend. Faithful, loyal, loving. Giving all. Asking nothing. In a few weeks you'll wonder how you ever lived without him."

Out of breath, she had to stop. If he was impressed, he hid it well. In fact there was a tinge of sardonic amusement in his eyes she didn't care for at all. Not that it mattered what he thought. She wasn't the issue here. Arthur was.

Karl Wagner looked from her to the dog as if he might say something, then merely nodded. His arm shot out and flexed. A wafer-thin gold watch worth a lifetime's supply of dog food apparently gave him his clue. "Molly, we have to hurry or you won't be able to get something for Nana."

Molly gave Arthur one last pat before she turned away and slipped her hand into her father's.

Failure was a dry well; disappointment the gravity pulling Jessica inexorably to the bottom. If she'd failed on her own account, she wouldn't have minded so much. But Arthur's life was in question here. Tears threw themselves against the muscles of her throat, wanting out. Agony drummed a finale in her ears.

"No."

The word held as much conviction as a solitary male chauvinist at a women's lib rally. She'd not only failed, but she'd broken every rule in the Humane Society book. José Garcia had warned her about this.

Rule number one was to be detached about the animal in your care.

Jessica hadn't been able to muster a trace of detachment after the first long look from Arthur's molasses eyes.

Rule number two was never force a pet on anyone. For it to work, the process had to be carefully thought out.

Jessica was a breath away from breaking that one, as well. She wanted to run after Molly and her father, beg them to think of taking Arthur home with them.

Irrational as the urge was, she couldn't even explain it to herself. Gut instinct again. That's what it was. She just knew that Arthur and the pair would do well together. It had to do with the gentleness with which Molly had patted Arthur, the love in the hazel eyes. Karl Wagner was right for Arthur, too, though he didn't seem to think so.

"It's something to do with his mouth," she explained to Arthur.

Jessica had studied mouths over the years. Thin-lipped ones belonged to people who had a tendency to miserliness. Too-full lips hinted at deeply sensual natures, except in her case—she was as sensual as a case of Granny Smith apples. Normal mouths, neither too thin nor too full, were a happy, balanced blend of everything. The right sort for Arthur. The right sort for *her*?

Unbidden, the memory of being scrutinized came to mind. Jessica shivered. She should have stopped for breakfast. Or made use of the break she'd been spelled for, by getting herself something to eat. Hunger was making her light-headed, playing strange games with her emotions.

"It's not as if I'm a kid," she elaborated to Arthur. "I'm a logical, clearheaded woman." That fact still didn't buy her insurance against a pair of laser eyes or account for why her heart felt as if it had been on a roller coaster all afternoon.

Chapter Two

At half-past three a woman in a fur jacket stopped by to talk about Arthur. Jessica took in thin lips, painted a deep fuchsia, the pretentiousness of the stranger's manner, and her hackles rose.

"Isn't he cute?" A blast of a hundred-and-twenty-dollar-an-ounce perfume hit Jessica. "I could use him in my commercials."

Jessica looked down at her shoes. A nightmare vision of Arthur perpetually on the end of a chain, being arranged in poses under the glare of camera lights all day, churned her stomach. His only purpose would be as a foil to this woman whose gravest concerns were the color of her toenails, the state of her hair.

Over Jessica's dead body.

"You don't want this dog," she said point-blank. "He's got a sullen nature."

"Oh, my!" The leather-skirted vision stepped back. Jessica's grip tightened on the collar, and Arthur cocked his head benignly. The model moved her million-dollar legs clear out of nipping range.

As the woman left without a backward glance, Jessica's gaze shifted to Arthur. Guilt throttled her like a choke chain.

"I couldn't let her have you," she said fiercely. "A life like that would be worse than—" she swallowed hard— "worse than..."

Jessica sighed. As usual she was guilty of leading with her heart. The mother-hen syndrome made her want to protect the whole world.

She'd probably scotched Arthur's only chance of having a home.

"Want to pack it in?"

Jessica looked at José Garcia and then around her. She was the only volunteer left of the twenty that had been there since eleven that morning. It was four o'clock. Nineteen animals had found new homes. The last one stretched his forepaws, gave an enormous sigh and put his head down. His unquestioning acceptance of whatever lay in store for him rekindled Jessica's fierce resolve, fanning it to blaze proportion.

"No," she said firmly. "There's still an hour left."

Under her stubborn stare, José Garcia's eyes dropped. He apparently didn't want to get into another argument with her.

Jessica blinked the tears away. She wasn't going to give up yet.

Concentrating on the thinning crowd, she picked out people who looked suitable and began sending out desperate telepathic messages to them. *Come here. Look into those soulful eyes. Do you know the difference a dog can make in your lives?* There seemed to be a breakdown in her ability to communicate mentally. No one stopped.

Jessica took Arthur for a brisk fifteen-minute walk outside at four-thirty. She was almost back to her spot when she noticed a familiar broad back approach José Garcia. Heart in mouth, Jessica picked up her pace. There could only be one reason they had returned.

"There was a teenage girl here earlier, about this high." Indignantly Jessica noted that his raised hand put her closer to four feet than five. "Dressed in really bright clothes, talks a lot." Red-hot color surged to her face. "She had a Great Dane with her. We were wondering if the dog's found a home."

"Looking for me?" Jessica's voice dripped honey. Laced with a lethal dose of arsenic.

He didn't look a whit abashed. Swung around and treated her to one of his gimlet glances.

"*Ms.* Hansen," inserted José Garcia helpfully, hitching up his pants, "is very knowledgeable about dogs. We are lucky she could help us today."

Jessica smiled her gratitude at the portly man, then looked coolly at Molly's father. Karl Wagner didn't look the least bit put out. One lofty eyebrow was his only reaction to the news she wasn't a teenager.

"You're still here!" Molly beamed. The smile slipped as she looked at Arthur. "Doesn't anyone want him?"

Jessica swallowed hard and mustered every drop of composure she had. Arthur's life was at stake here. That took precedence over wounded pride. "Not so far."

"Molly, I'm going to pick up my book." Karl Wagner's words extinguished hope completely. "Do you want to stay here?"

Molly nodded. "Yes, please."

Why had he come back if he wasn't interested in Arthur? Jessica didn't glance up as she sensed him walk away. José Garcia retreated to his folding table and began shuffling papers. A quarter to five. Her heart plummeted.

"How old is Arthur?" Molly asked.

"About two years old, they think."

Talking would help speed the remaining time. Tomorrow she would think up some new way of helping Arthur. All she wanted to do now was go home and have a good cry. Maybe it would lessen the pressure in her chest. It had been a rotten day from start to finish.

"Human years?"

"Human years," agreed Jessica. Considering each human year was seven years of a dog's life, Arthur was fourteen. In his prime. "Great Danes age a little faster than other breeds, though."

"Aren't some people mean?" Molly patted Arthur's head. "If you belonged to me, I would never leave you behind." The girl's hand suddenly stilled. She turned to Jessica, face riddled with excitement. "Can I have him?"

"Not unless your parents want him, too," Jessica said firmly.

Molly didn't reply. There was something about the faraway look in her eyes that Jessica could only classify as a Napoleonic gleam. In one as young as Molly, it could mean anything.

The father was coming out of the bookstore. Jessica's stomach muscles clenched as he neared. War was about to be declared. And she was on the wrong side this time. She kept her gaze riveted on Molly and Arthur.

"Hi, Uncle Karl!"

Uncle Karl.

For a second the world tilted. Colors whirled around her. Red—the explosion of shock. Green—the unbelievable happening. Golden yellow—promise of happiness.

"Molly, we have to go now or we won't have time to get your present."

Molly didn't budge. She tilted her head, and Jessica was reminded of a frigate going to war.

"Uncle Karl, I want this dog."

Surprise dropped Jessica's jaw at the same instant that Uncle Karl's dark brows snapped together. It was a moment before she absorbed the import of Molly's words.

"What did you say?"

"I want Arthur."

"You can't have this dog. He's huge." Uncle Karl glared at the world in general, Jessica in particular.

He thinks I put the idea into Molly's head.

Jessica tilted her chin so quickly her earrings swung to and fro as she glared back at him. Of all the nerve! He jumped to conclusions faster than she did.

"I know he's huge." Molly's matter-of-fact voice snapped the thread of tension. "That's what I like about him."

The well-cut lips tightened ominously as he said firmly, "You can't have him. Henley Apartment Complex doesn't allow dogs, remember? Where would you keep him?"

"At your house?" The guileless smile took Jessica's breath away. Molly was clearly a tactician of tremendous skill.

"Molly, *I* don't want a dog." Jessica's heart sank. He sounded stern and implacable. Maybe she'd been mistaken about the kind mouth. "Even if I did, I wouldn't pick one this big."

"You said I could pick out a present for Valentine's Day at the mall." The sigh and the dropped lids conveyed disillusionment perfectly. Molly shrugged with adult indifference. "Well, if you can't keep your word, I guess you can't."

Move over, Sarah Bernhardt. Molly's here now.

Her uncle looked as if someone had flung a glass of ice water in his face.

"Wha—?" Realization dawned, and he said defensively, "I promised you a present, not an animal the size of a house."

Molly's mouth tightened exactly like her uncle's. Jessica's insides shouted up a storm as she watched the pair.

"Grown-ups know best about these things," Jessica inserted gently. Which earned her another fiery look from *Uncle* Karl. One would think she was championing Molly's cause. She was, in her heart, of course, but for Arthur's future it was more important to have everybody want him.

Molly didn't say a word. She didn't have to. Her expression clearly implied her opinion of adults who didn't keep promises.

One hand raked through the thatch of black hair, reducing it to disorder. He was definitely not happy about this turn of events.

"Molly, when I mentioned a gift, I meant something you could keep with you, like a doll, or a dress." His face blanched as Arthur stretched. "Or a VCR for your room?"

Jessica's mouth twitched. He must really be getting desperate. Video recorders cost hundreds of dollars.

"You gave me a VCR for Christmas, remember?" Molly said reasonably.

Frustration increased tenfold on his face, "So I did. Well, how about a telephone of your very own? You'd like that, wouldn't you?"

"Maybe when I'm a teenager," the terror said kindly. "I'm only eight. Let's go home, Uncle Karl. I'm very tired."

He took a step forward, stopped, stared from Molly to the dog. A gamut of emotions chased across his face.

"I'm a dentist. I don't know anything about dogs. I don't have time for one."

The litany didn't seem directed at human ears.

A dentist. Jessica's pulse accelerated. Based on what her dentist charged every time he asked her to open her mouth, money certainly wasn't one of Uncle Karl's problems. And that mouth. She checked again quickly. Yes, there was hope. Excitement spiraled within her.

Come on, Molly.

"You'll only have to keep him till we get our own house," said Molly reasonably. "Dad said it wouldn't take more than five to six weeks for escrow, and they've promised me a dog." Turning to Jessica, she said, "We've just moved from New York to be near Uncle Karl. That's how come we're in an apartment."

She'd neatly piled one more layer of guilt on her uncle's shoulders. Jessica dared not look at him. The UN had desperate need of diplomats like Molly.

Pulling a wallet out of his hip pocket, her uncle held out a five-dollar bill to Molly. "See the ice-cream place?" he inquired, pointing to a spot two stores away. "Treat yourself to a cone and then sit on that bench till I call you." He pointed to a wooden bench surrounded by artistically massed greenery, out of hearing range. "I'm going to call your parents and then make a decision."

Molly nodded angelically and set off.

Jessica braced herself as the angry giant returned after the phone call. She could almost see the smoke billowing from his nostrils.

"As I said before," he threw at her repressively, "I don't want a dog."

Behind her, José Garcia snapped a case shut and cleared his throat. Arthur's time had run out. She'd failed, after all.

"If I do this, it will be for Molly."

Surprise jerked Jessica's head up.

She had to repeat the words to herself to be sure she'd heard them right. Molly's parents must have agreed to Molly's having Arthur. Ignoring the herd of butterflies performing acrobatics in her stomach, Jessica smiled widely. "You won't regret it."

He looked at her swimmy eyes, and a spark shot out of his own as he smiled. The first real smile he'd given her. Not rescuing-angel smile, not kind-and-caring smile. This was big-league. Man-woman. Joy slipped out of Jessica's heart, wrapped them in a layer of emotion so thick the rest of the world faded away. Karl Wagner's glance slipped to her mouth. Time missed a beat.

A loudly cleared throat startled Jessica. José Garcia was getting restless. It was past five o'clock.

She bent to pat Arthur. It was as good a way of hiding her hot face as any. No one had ever told her a smile could induce cerebral paralysis.

"Tell me what you know about the dog's history."

"He was found two weeks ago, starving, abandoned." The well-molded lips tightened. Jessica was reminded of the way he'd dealt with the two delinquents. Karl Wagner had no use for cruelty. "He's two years old and in excellent physical condition. Great Danes are very good with children, very amenable. He won't be any trouble." Honesty took over. "Any dog does require a certain amount of care and attention." A quick glance at his face as he looked toward his niece wasn't encouraging. There was still some indecision there. Scared that he was slipping through her fingers, Jessica laid her hand on his arm. "Would you like to pat him?"

He looked down pointedly at the hand resting on his forearm. Conscious of nails bitten to the quick, of being carried away, Jessica snatched her hand back.

Going down on his haunches, Molly's uncle put his hand out to the dog. Arthur lifted his head and stared at him, then gave a mournful sigh and settled down on his front paws.

"It will take a while to gain his trust and affection. He's been badly hurt by his last owner's desertion." There was nothing she could do about the tremor in her voice when she thought of *how* Arthur had been left. It earned her another sharp glance.

"Uncle Karl, have you made up your mind?" Molly was back with a dripping ice-cream cone in one hand. Evidently she didn't feel her uncle had to be obeyed to the letter.

His hesitation reminded Jessica of a thoroughbred balking at the gate.

"I don't know much about dogs," he said cautiously, like a man who had to feel his way out of a sticky situation.

"There isn't that much to know," Jessica said quickly. "They are a lot like children. You learn as you go along." It sounded like a power statement. Her mother always said that. "He's housebroken, so he definitely won't give you any trouble in that area. Besides, if he has a doghouse in the yard and the use of the garage when the weather's bad, he needn't come into the house at all." Considering what her dentist charged just to look into her mouth, Jessica was sure Molly's uncle could afford to hire help. "You could pay a teenager to walk him during the week if you didn't have the time yourself. I know a friend's daughter who charges a dollar-fifty a day for walking an elderly neighbor's dog. She also cleans the dog's dishes and sets out his food."

Something flickered in Uncle Karl's eyes. Lack of interest? Jessica wished she'd something more to hold him with.

One-inch-long eyelashes. Legs like the model's. Fear inserted a quaver in her voice. "He'd be a fine friend."

"I'd take care of him, Uncle Karl." Molly clung earnestly to his large hand. "I'll give him a bath every week, and you can have all my pocket money for feeding him. Mommy says she'll increase my allowance if I keep my room clean. I'll give you that money, too. You only have to keep him till we find a house. It won't be for long. Please? Pretty please with macadamia nuts on it?"

So he liked macadamia nuts. She would ship him ten pounds every month. If only he would take Arthur.

Each moment of silence was a weighted force crushing hope. Jessica's heart sank. Maybe she'd been wrong about the mouth. Maybe the thought of the expense of paying someone to care for the dog was too much for Molly's uncle. The fact that he had money didn't necessarily mean he wanted to spend it.

Behind her, José Garcia was packing up, a definite hint that he couldn't let her have any more time. Five-fifteen. Desperation clutched at Jessica's throat.

"If lack of time is all that's worrying you, I can come by every evening, walk him and put out his food," she said urgently. It was the least she could do for Arthur.

"You won't have to do a thing, Uncle Karl," Molly seconded seriously. "Jessica and I will do it all."

Jessica crossed her fingers behind her back.

"I'll give you my number. That way, if you ever need any help with him, you can call me. I have quite a bit of experience with dogs."

Her eyes were fixed on Molly, but her words were meant for Karl. *Please.* She appealed again to the powers that be. *Oh, please! Don't let him back out now.*

A long pause, and then just as her heart began to scrunch up with the pain of disappointment, she heard him say, "We'll take him."

Her smile almost split her face. Molly squealed and wrapped herself around her uncle's waist. Jessica struggled with the impulse to follow suit.

"I'm going to call you Arthur, too," Molly announced to the dog, surprising Jessica. "You belong to me now, boy. You're never going to be lonely again."

Success was an unfurling rose, happiness the early-morning dew on it. Tears of relief flooded Jessica's eyes again. Arthur had a home and a new owner whose heart matched his size. Karl Wagner, she was sure, would eventually grow to love the dog.

José came up to them, the beaming smile on his face indicating how much he liked happy endings.

"José Garcia, with the L.A. County Humane Society, sir. If you're sure about wanting the dog, I'll explain about costs and shots and so on."

The Humane Society had a minimum charge of twenty dollars for the dogs adopted, based on the premise that people were more careful with something they paid for.

"Karl Wagner." Molly's uncle shook the official's hand. "Yes, I'm quite sure."

Surreptitiously Jessica put a hand up to the corner of one eye to blot a tear. Stealing a glance upward, she saw Molly's uncle watching her and blushed. He looked at her for a long moment before following José to the folding table to take care of the paperwork.

Jessica took a deep breath. The man's eyes were a lethal weapon against which she had no defense.

"Dogs are a big responsibility." Jessica dragged her mind back to the present, launched into the speech they had been asked to include in their sales pitch. "It wouldn't be fair to take Arthur if you don't intend to keep him. Dogs get attached to people, and if they're abandoned, they're heartbroken."

"I know." Molly nodded seriously. "My grandma is from England. She told me about Greyfriars Bobby, the dog who stayed on his master's grave for years and years. I won't ever give Arthur up."

"Does your uncle have a big yard?"

Molly nodded again. "Do you know where Jacaranda Meadows is?" she asked Jessica. "It's a new development right off the freeway, about ten minutes from here. Uncle Karl bought a house there. He has a huge yard, plus half a hillside."

Jessica blinked. Jacaranda Meadows was only five minutes away from her apartment. She'd gone there last year to look at the model homes when the development had won national acclaim as best master-planned community of the year. The estate homes with view lots were spectacular. Arthur was definitely moving up.

"Will you come and help us pick out his things?" Molly asked. "I'm not sure what he needs."

The hair on Jessica's nape warned of Karl Wagner's return. She turned to watch lean strong fingers fold a piece of paper and put it into a leather wallet. Had he heard his niece's request?

"We have to get a dish and some food, Uncle Karl," Molly informed her uncle. "Hurry before the pet store closes."

"I'm ready, Molly."

"Will you come and help us?" Molly asked again.

Jessica looked at Karl Wagner. Now that the decision was made, he seemed reconciled to having Arthur. That was good. Given time, he might even begin to care for the dog.

"I can sit in the car with Arthur," he said, one side of his mouth quirked upward, "and you two can pick out whatever he needs."

Jessica hesitated. It was as much of an invitation as she was going to get from him. She squared her shoulders and said crisply, "There's a store quite close by. Let me give you directions. I'll meet you there."

As Jessica slid behind the wheel of her secondhand car she took a deep breath. And a few more. She was doing this for Arthur. And her imagination better believe that.

Half an hour later they stood by the car again, purchases completed.

"You have all you need for the present," Jessica said as Karl got out of the car and put the packages into the trunk. "Molly's going to feed Arthur tonight and tomorrow. I'll be over Monday evening." Jessica had to tilt her neck way back to look at him. In the gloaming she couldn't see his face clearly. Holding out the change from the hundred-dollar bill he'd given her, along with the cash receipt, Jessica was very conscious of his nearness.

"Thanks for helping Molly pick out the things." The warmth in his voice sent tiny tremors through Jessica's body.

"Well, I guess I'd better be going." Wanting to was no excuse for lingering.

"How about dinner?" The question caught her by surprise. "I noticed a place called Kim's Soup and Sandwiches across the street. Would you care to join us? I know Molly's hungry."

Jessica hesitated. He probably wanted to discuss times she could go over to care for Arthur and so on. Her stomach growled an urgent reminder that she was starving. "A sandwich does sound nice."

Molly asked to eat in the car. Jessica suspected Arthur was going to share the requested double burger, but she didn't say anything. A little spoiling was exactly what Arthur deserved.

Karl chose a tiny table by a window through which he could keep an eye on Molly. Jessica felt a surge of electricity move up her spine and interfere with her breathing as they sat down. Maybe this wasn't such a good idea. Maybe she should have gone straight home.

This close he seemed to shut out the world. He took big clean bites and chewed quietly. He didn't talk with his mouth full. He didn't ...

For heaven's sake! she scolded herself. She was really going overboard with this awareness thing today. Who nominated you Emily Post's assistant? Concentrate on your meal.

"Whatever you may think, I didn't talk Molly into adopting Arthur." She hated untidy ends and she wanted to clear up this one.

"I know. My niece has a mind of her own. It's just that for a few moments there I felt trapped."

She could understand that. "He won't be any trouble, you'll see," she said comfortingly.

Karl Wagner flicked her with his gimlet gaze. "So, how does it feel to be victorious?"

"Victorious?"

"You found Arthur a new owner. José Garcia told me how you championed his cause, what it meant to you to find a home for him. You're a fighter, aren't you?"

Color stained Jessica's face. The old blabbermouth. She had a good mind not to take José the bowl of special chili she'd promised him. "Arthur deserves another chance. I only wanted to make sure he got it."

"What would have happened if he'd been returned to the shelter today?"

"He would have been put to sleep." Jessica swallowed the lump in her throat. "The length of time they keep the animals depends on space. Arthur's been there three weeks already."

A silence ensued. And grew.

"You won't regret taking him. He's a wonderful dog," Jessica repeated.

Narrow prisms of light reached out to her from Karl's dark eyes. Jessica felt her mind pull up anchor, drift away to a distant galaxy where the sky was silk, each new sensation a star.

"I don't think I will, at that."

"I beg your pardon?" What had they been talking about?

Karl wiped his mouth, crumpled the napkin and tossed it into the empty box in front of him. "Never mind. You've had a long day. You look half-asleep. Shall we go?"

Half asleep wasn't what she wanted to look like. She wanted glamorous, gorgeous, *unforgettable*.

"I haven't finished my sandwich." Jessica took another bite, chewed slowly. One didn't hurry a dream along.

"Should I get some meat and a bone for Arthur from the supermarket tomorrow?"

"No." Jessica vetoed the suggestion immediately. "Raw meat is bad for dogs. It carries all kinds of bacteria that cause bad stomach infections. Real bones are out, too. When dogs chew them, bits break off and damage their intestines. Natural bones wear out a dog's teeth, as well. There's a nylon bone in the bag that Molly can let him have. Surveys show that's the best kind for a pet."

"Do you have a dog of your own?"

"Not now. I live in an apartment that doesn't allow pets. As a kid, though, I can't remember a time when I didn't have a dog."

"A Great Dane?"

"No. A Benji type first, called Tramp, then a black-and-white mongrel called Trucker."

The trouble with fast food was it disappeared too quickly. One couldn't chew forever. Jessica closed her empty box, emptiness pooling inside. It was time for the last curtain call.

Outside she thanked Karl Wagner for her dinner, patted Arthur on the head and exchanged a few words with Molly through the window of the Audi.

"Bye, Jessica. I'll take good care of Arthur. Don't you worry about him," promised Molly solemnly.

Jessica felt the prick of tears behind her lids. "I know you will, Molly."

A cold mist of loneliness that had nothing to do with leaving Arthur accompanied her home. There was no reason a successful day should have left her so empty.

The telephone startled her awake at six the next morning. Jessica opened one eye to glare at the invention balefully. The caller had better have a good reason for disturbing her. She loved sleeping late on the weekends. She'd sacrificed Saturday with no second thoughts. She wasn't about to do the same with Sunday.

"Jessica, we can't find Arthur anywhere." Molly's hurriedly caught-back sob held pure pathos. "I think he's run away."

"I'll be right over." Adrenaline flooded her system, chasing out the last traces of sleepiness. *Oh, Arthur.* "Give me directions, will you?"

Karl Wagner came on the line. There was nothing in his voice that revealed how he felt about the situation. Jessica scribbled down directions, thankful he was saving his comments for when she got there, and flew into the bathroom.

It wasn't till she got off the freeway at Jacaranda Meadows that she realized the orange wraparound skirt she had grabbed, and yesterday's red shirt, made her look like a rotten egg yolk.

Oh, well. It didn't really matter. What mattered was finding Arthur and convincing Molly's uncle that the dog wouldn't make a habit of running away.

She barely stopped the car when Molly flung herself into her arms and lifted a tear-blotched face. "I woke at five and went down, and he wasn't anywhere. Uncle Karl has helped me look everywhere." She gulped back a hiccuping sob.

"Shh, it's all right. We'll find him." Jessica hugged the girl to her, gently caressed her head.

What on earth was she going to say to Karl Wagner? Arthur had already proved wrong every word she'd uttered yesterday. Jessica winced, recalling her exact words. *No trouble at all. A fine friend. Worth his weight in gold.*

Arthur had let her down badly.

Chapter Three

Over Molly's head Jessica looked at Karl Wagner. The rumpled hair, sleep-tousled eyes, the blue tinge of his chin, made him look heart-stirringly human. He was still in his pajama top, but had pulled on jeans over the bottoms. The beige material peeped out over the waistband of his jeans. In the V of the unbuttoned top nestled a clump of curly black hair. It didn't take a psychic to guess he'd dressed in a hurry.

Jessica sucked in a deep breath and blinked. She hadn't come here to stand and stare at the man. "Let me call the Humane Society first, then we'll go look for him," she told an overwrought Molly.

The official who answered the call at the Pomona Humane Society said no one had reported spotting a runaway Great Dane yet. Yes, the woman would get back to them immediately if someone did. Yes, she would make a note of it for the officials who came in later.

Jessica sighed as she hung up. Molly's chin wobbled ominously. She'd caught the gist of the conversation.

"Show me around outside," Jessica said gently.

Molly's description had been accurate. The enormous yard wrapped the house on three sides. On two sides it was walled with concrete and stone. The back went straight out for fifty yards and then sloped gently to a wrought-iron fence. Beyond the iron railings were huge clumps of oleander bushes. Karl Wagner certainly liked his privacy.

Jessica whistled and called alternately as she walked toward the railings. "Here, Arthur. Come here, boy."

There really weren't any hiding places in the yard itself for a dog his size. A stretch of grass, beautifully landscaped, low bushes and flower beds, a winding path. To one side a miniature waterfall gurgled into a lily pond. Medium-sized fruit trees punctuated the gentle slope of the hillside. Jessica walked to the bottom of the hill and raised her voice.

There was a scrambling sound from behind the oleanders. Heart thumping, Jessica called again, "Here, Arthur. Come on, boy. Come on."

The rustling was repeated. Molly ran past her just as the big dog wiggled under the fence. Jessica followed, noticing the pile of dirt beside the freshly tunneled hole. Going down on her knees beside the dog, Jessica put a hand on his side and scolded softly, "Where have you been?"

It wasn't exactly an auspicious first beginning. What had Molly said? She'd woken at five to check on him? Jessica groaned silently. Less than twenty-four hours, and already Arthur was making waves.

Molly sobbed into Arthur's neck. "Don't you ever, *ever* do that again, you bad dog."

Jessica's own eyes flooded at the love threaded through the relief in Molly's voice. Apparently Arthur sensed it, too. A huge tongue came out, and he licked Molly's tears.

"Did you see that?" The little girl's tone held awe; her tears magically stemmed. "He likes me! I thought he ran away because he was frightened of me."

"Not of you," Jessica said gently. "Just of the new place, of another move."

"Let's go back to the house." Karl Wagner's voice was gruff, not unkind. "The grass is still wet out here."

"He's afraid and disoriented—that's why he ran away and hid." Jessica plunged into Arthur's defense as soon as Molly was out of earshot. "It's going to take a while for him to settle down. He really won't be any trouble once he gets used to your place. In fact it might be a good idea to tether him to the end of a long rope for a day or two till he gets used to his new home. That way you won't have to go through this again. I can stop off at the hardware store for some rope and come back later."

Aware she was babbling, Jessica stopped and stole a look at Karl. A corner of his mouth quirked upward. Relief swamped Jessica. He wasn't angry.

"I have some rope in the garage," he responded quietly. "If you will show Molly how to tether him, I'll fix some breakfast for all of us. Tomorrow I'll get somebody to fix the fence at the back so he can't get under it again."

Jessica sat on the deck and sipped the coffee Karl brought out. Molly was beside a tethered Arthur, leaning against his broad side. Her clear young voice carried into the morning air as she explained to Arthur why he had to be tied. The fifteen-foot rope Karl had produced ensured Arthur ample freedom, access to sun, shade, two dishes of water, his bone, a ball and what looked like a piece of carpeting to lie on.

Life should be so good to every dog.

Jessica looked around her appreciatively. The redwood deck was raised four feet off the ground and ran the width of the house. Steps separated it from the lawn. Huge white tubs sported bursts of spring color at each corner. Somewhere in the trees, a pair of birds twittered furiously. The rays of the rising sun shot the sky with molten gold.

An enchanted morning. Jessica closed her eyes, took a deep breath, ordered her pulse to calm down.

She wasn't a lump of clay to be so easily impressed. The fact that Karl Wagner was a good-looking, sensitive human being was no reason to fall in love with him. There was more to love and marriage than just "getting your man." Her mother and four sisters didn't agree. In their family a woman was considered lucky when a man took an interest in her. If that man had a steady income and was nice looking, wedding bells were in order. They had rung many times already. But not for Jessica. Jessica wanted something more. She just wasn't sure what. It had to do with fairy godmothers, a special feeling, *magic*.

"Breakfast's almost ready. Let me show you where the bathroom is."

Jessica jumped and pushed her glasses up. How long had he been there? Had he seen her mooning-like-a-sick-cow look? Leaving her damp shoes on the mat outside the patio door, she stepped into the house. He'd taken a few minutes to shower and shave. His light brown slacks and fawn T-shirt made her feel like a bag lady. The light scent of sandalwood drifted to Jessica from Karl. She took a deep, greedy breath.

They were in an enormous family room separated from a gourmet kitchen by an eating island. The hallmark of designer decorating was everywhere. Jessica followed Karl down a small hallway that veered to the right.

Inside the bathroom, she leaned against the door. Her reflection in the gorgeous mirror over the gold-streaked ivory washbasin was the only thing out of place. It didn't seem possible, but she looked plainer than ever this morning. Jessica washed her hands and contemplated having a perm. It might make her look more interesting.

Wiping her hands nervously on a velour hand towel edged with a satin border of scalloped sea shells, checking to make sure she hadn't left any dirt marks, Jessica grinned ruefully. It would need a whole lot more than a perm to make her over. It would need plastic surgery.

The redwood table had been set by the time she went outside again. A covered dish, three glasses of what looked like freshly squeezed orange juice and a pot of coffee rested on a smooth oak tray. A wicker basket held bran muffins ensconced in a napkin. Curls of butter in a crystal dish, three kinds of preserves. Karl Wagner didn't do things by halves.

"Come and sit down. Molly wants to have a picnic next to Arthur."

She wondered how old he was, why he was watching the fiesty little girl this weekend, whether it threw a spanner in the leisure routine of an eligible bachelor.

It's none of your business.

Jessica shook her head. She could always rely on her conscience to clear her head fast.

"Is everything all right? Don't you like eggs?"

Aware he was waiting for her to start eating, Jessica picked up her fork. "Everything's fine."

They ate in silence for a while, then she asked, "Where are Molly's parents?"

Karl looked at her, laid his knife down before saying slowly, "My sister, Andy, Molly's mother, is in the last trimester of a difficult pregnancy. Carrying the baby to full term means Andy has to stay in bed. Jim, my brother-in-law, is a chartered public accountant who's just opened his own office in Walnut. He has to work long hours, besides coping with all the work at home. It doesn't give him much time to do things with Molly. Andy and Jim are both worried about how all this is affecting her. I try to help by having her here as much as possible, doing things with her. She's a neat kid."

"Yes, she is." Jessica wiped her mouth on a snowy-white napkin, glad she wasn't wearing any lipstick. That explained his capitulation over Arthur. She'd wondered about that. Despite his mouth, Jessica didn't think either Molly's tactics or her own powers of persuasion could influence Karl Wagner. He didn't look the malleable kind. But he'd realized a dog could make a difference to Molly.

"Molly, precocious as she is, worries about her mother," Karl went on. "I'm hoping weekends here, especially now she has Arthur, will help."

Jessica didn't know any other single man who would do so much for a niece. He must be very close to his sister. The way he was with Molly made it even harder to figure out why he was still single.

Jessica swallowed. It was none of her business. General conversation was all that was called for, not speculation about the man's private life.

"Nice place you have here."

"I like it." He sounded as detached about it as he did about most things.

"Do you live here alone?"

He raised an eyebrow, and hot color flooded her cheeks. She'd done it again. Charged into a private part of his life that was none of her business.

"What I mean is, your house seems so huge for one person, and it must need quite a bit of cleaning and . . ."

And you'd better shut up long enough to get your foot out of your mouth, Jessica Hansen.

"I like space." Jessica couldn't understand the gleam in Karl's eyes. He looked more amused than irritated. "The house is a good investment. A cleaning crew comes in once a week to give the place a once-over. For the rest of the time, I like being by myself."

Jessica forked up a small mountain of scrambled eggs and put it in her mouth. It was one way of keeping it closed. After a while she felt his eyes on her and looked up.

"What's wrong?" he asked.

"Wrong?" She sipped her coffee to clear her throat, then said, "Nothing. Why?"

"You've been quiet—" he looked at his watch "—for all of two minutes. Why?"

That hurt. Her next words were frosty. "Whatever you may think, Dr. Wagner, I don't babble continuously."

"Karl," he corrected. "We've been through too much to be formal, Jessica."

"Karl." The way he said her name made it sound beautiful. His had emerged a croak.

"You must live close by to have gotten here so quickly this morning."

"Three miles away. I rent an apartment in Clearview."

"That's convenient." His gaze went to the picture Molly made on the grass by Arthur. She was leaning against the Great Dane, feeding him tidbits off her plate. Jessica looked at Karl. He didn't seem to mind. It was all working out well. With a little bit of luck, there'd be no further mishaps. Jessica smiled just as Karl turned and looked at her.

"What would you have done if we lived farther away? Would you still have offered to look after Arthur?"

Jessica nodded. "Yes. Driving long distances is a way of life in California. A little while more behind the wheel wouldn't really make that much difference."

It wouldn't do to let him know she avoided freeway driving as much as she could. She even took a company van pool to work and back each day.

"Do you work close by?" he asked.

The question seemed harmless enough. "I work for California Electronics. The company is based twenty miles away." She shifted in her chair, uneasy under his intense gaze.

"How long does the commute take?" Karl broke off a small bunch of grapes and put one in his mouth.

"About forty-five minutes each way in rush hour traffic." She stared at the bunch he placed on her plate. She couldn't remember asking for any.

"What do you do?" was his next question.

"I'm a computer programmer. I work in payroll."

"I got a PC last year, but I just use it for letters," Karl offered. "Still haven't had time to explore its full potential."

About to offer to show him what else he could do with it, Jessica closed her mouth just in time, adopting her giant clam look. She wasn't going to make the mistake of giving this man the impression she was trying to instigate further meetings.

Busy with her own thoughts, Jessica jumped a foot when Karl touched her. She stared down, hypnotized by the finger trailing across the back of her hand.

"So small." His touch brought a million nerve endings to life. "And yet so strong." Picking up her hand, he looked at her nails. "Why do you bite them?"

Jessica had to open her mouth twice before sound emerged. "It's a bad habit. I read a lot and I'm always chewing on my nails when I do that."

A slight frown crossed his face. "It's also a nervous gesture. Tell me, Jessica Hansen, what makes you nervous? Boyfriend problems?"

Other people blushed a delicate pink. Jessica's blushes were classified beetroot red.

"I don't have a boyfriend," she said shortly.

He was doing it to her again. Making her feel at a disadvantage. And she wished he would let go of her hand.

His hold tightened, almost involuntarily. "No boyfriend? It's hard to believe some man hasn't staked a claim on you yet."

Staked a claim indeed! Hadn't the man had his head out of peoples' mouths long enough to hear about women's lib?

"It's a two-way thing," she said stiffly.

"Ah." His thumb caressed the mound under her thumb. The Venus mound. "So it is. Tell me, Jessica, have you ever experienced this, er, two-way thing?"

The quirk infuriated her. Jessica went hot and then cold. How dare he laugh at her? How dare she *enjoy* it?

"No." Speech was becoming difficult. His touch was interfering with rational thinking.

"Uncle Karl, do you think Jessica can come with us to buy the book about Great Danes and some rawhide bones for Arthur?" Molly leaned against his chair and blew on her fringe.

"Why don't you ask Jessica if she wants to?" His expression gave nothing away.

Jessica stood up and picked up her bag. "I'm sorry, Molly, but I have a whole heap of things to do today." A whole day in Karl Wagner's company was more than she could handle in her present state of mind. "Why don't you call me when you get back and tell me how Arthur's doing?"

Cleaning her apartment didn't take long. Jessica had a system worked out. Vacuum, dust, clean kitchen, clean bathroom. She saved laundry for Sundays, preferring to take it to a Laundromat and read while it got done rather than make numerous trips up and down to the laundry room by the apartment office.

As Jessica mopped the bathroom floor, her mind wandered back to that morning. The picture of sun-warmed eyes laughing at her wasn't easy to dispel. The mop moved back and forth even more vigorously. Dr. Karl Wagner wasn't her type at all.

Impulse moved her to the mirror. Taking off her glasses, she brushed orange-gold blush over her cheeks, dabbing a spot on her chin like the girl who had once done her face had demonstrated. A peachy lipstick, some mascara, dark eyeshadow, and she stood back.

Hands on hips, she practiced a sway that would bring a man to his knees. It made her look like a sparrow with gout. Jessica sighed. What couldn't be improved had to be left strictly alone.

By midafternoon she was settled on her plaid couch, a bowl of hot buttered popcorn beside her. There was a Western she'd taped midweek that she wanted to watch. With her hand on the remote control, about to switch on her television set, Jessica paused. Her nails did look awful. Setting the remote control down, she reached for the telephone book.

The next morning Jessica almost decided to join the group that wanted a law passed against working on Mondays.

She overslept and arrived at the park-and-ride area just in time to glimpse the receding taillights of the company van. Her car needed gas if she was to drive herself to work. By the time she filled the tank, her hands were smelly and she had a smear of dirt on the cuff of her ice blue blouse. The commute to work in stop-and-go traffic tied her up in knots, as usual.

A note from her supervisor awaited her on her desk, asking Jessica to come to the woman's office if Jessica ever got in. Below the flourish of Margo Hanes's name was the time Jessica was supposed to be at her desk by each day: 8 a.m.

Jessica made a face at the note. "You're lucky I'm here at all," she muttered as she put her bag away.

Margo wasn't in her office, but there was plenty to do. Slipping off her jacket, Jessica switched on her computer terminal and got right down to work. One small slip had her going over her work till her eyes began to burn and the morning's promised headache became a thundering reality.

The telephone rang, and she snatched it up. "Jessica Hansen."

"Ms. Hansen? I'm Edna Lucas, Dr. Wagner's office manager."

"Yes?" Jessica rolled her eyes in silent prayer. Not another Arthur crisis. Margo stood at the door of her office, making imperious signs with a crooked finger. Jessica held up a hand to show she'd seen her.

"Dr. Wagner asked me to pass on a message," the rich, syrupy voice went on. "He has hired a boy to feed Arthur and take him for a walk every day, so you don't have to bother going over there."

"Thanks for letting me know." Naturally he was too busy to call her himself. It shouldn't hurt, but it did.

On her way to Margo's office, Jessica told herself it was great news. She could read between the lines as clearly as anyone else. Karl Wagner could handle it from here, on his own. Which was a good thing. It left her more free time, a precious commodity in southern California life-styles. She could always find out how Arthur was doing from Molly.

That particular door hadn't even made a noise as it had slammed shut in her face.

Margo wanted her to work late. Normally the thought of the extra money she'd make working overtime would have cheered Jessica up. Today it just added to the time before she could go home and eat a pound of chocolates.

It was eight-thirty before Margo was satisfied with the figures they had come up with. The half-empty freeways made up for the morning's congestion. Jessica kept her eyes on the road, but allowed her thoughts to wander.

She'd never had a burning ambition to be anything. Unlike David, who had wanted to study medicine from when he was ten. When their father's bypass surgery had imposed a severe strain on the family finances, David had mentioned dropping out of premed courses and taking a job. Jessica had vetoed the idea immediately, interrupted her own studies, got a full-time job delivering pizza and insisted David remain in school. She could help at home, and the money set aside for her college expenses would go toward her father's medical bills. Everybody had pitched in financially, and it wasn't long before Jessica had found she could go back to school. It had taken another year of evening classes at the local community college to qualify her for an entry-level position in computer programming. When a job fair in Oakland had netted her this job, it had provided her with the excuse she needed to leave home. She'd worked at CE for four years now.

On honest days Jessica admitted she was marking time. Waiting for what, she wasn't quite sure. There were just moments when an ache inside her made her feel she wanted more out of life than a good job.

She turned into the apartment complex, found a parking spot and ordered herself not to be silly. Tiredness always triggered the kind of soul-searching she had no answers for.

Bath and bed seemed all Jessica had energy left for when she entered her apartment. But that wasn't the way it worked. After changing into sweatpants and a T-shirt, Jessica switched on the television set and her video recorder.

Exercise was something she couldn't skimp on, late though it was. The benefits were too great to pass up. Maybe today it would help her regain control of her mind, as well.

She was into the leg lifts when the telephone interrupted. Jessica tried ignoring it, but it was no use. It went on and on. It had to be David. No one else was that persistent.

"Do you know what that mutt has done now?" Karl Wagner asked without any preamble.

"What?" Jessica reached for the towel she'd set down on the arm of her couch and wiped her neck. Something warned her it wasn't as simple as running away.

"He has dug holes all over the backyard." The suppressed anger in his voice seemed to leap out of the phone straight at Jessica. "Moon craters. And they are filled with water. My entire backyard is covered with miniature lakes."

"Wonder how he could have filled them with water?" The only possibility that occurred to her was ludicrous. Even a Great Dane as large as Arthur couldn't fill holes by answering nature's call.

"How he...?" Irritation dark and intense replaced the split-second query in Karl's voice. "Why do you always go off on a tangent? Do you know how much it cost to landscape that yard?" Exacerbation was the only word that aptly described Karl Wagner's tone. Beyond rage... beyond listening.

"He's lonely and he's scared," said Jessica reasonably. "I hope you didn't yell at him and scare him further."

There was a deadly silence for a few seconds. Karl Wagner's next words were dropped like stones into a pond. "I won't put up with this."

The implacable tone pushed a panic button. "What do you mean?" Jessica couldn't keep the fear out of her voice. "You can't take him back now. You know his time is up at the shelter. He'll just be put to sleep. Can you live with that?''

"Don't you dare lay a guilt trip on me." The clipped tone confirmed Molly's uncle was past persuasion. Into cold resolve. ''I get enough of that from Molly as it is. I will not put up with destruction of my property.''

Rage, pure and red-hot, shot through Jessica's veins. "That's right," she snapped, blinking furiously. "Your house is an investment, isn't it? I suppose the landscaping has enhanced its value. Tell me how much your property's worth, Dr. Wagner. Four hundred thousand? Five? Six? What chance does a living, breathing dog have against the value of your investment?''

"It's not that—"

But Jessica had heard enough. She was on a roll here and she let anger sweep her along to the crest. "Maybe that is what's best for Arthur, as well," she flung at him. "He would be miserable living with a person so set in his ways that he cannot stand any disruptions."

"I'm not—"

But she wouldn't give any quarter. "I was wrong about you. I thought you had a kind mouth, a big heart. I don't know why I jumped to that conclusion. I'll pick up Arthur at eight tomorrow and take him back to the shelter."

It gave Jessica the greatest satisfaction to bang down the receiver childishly.

And one and two and one and two. The model's vacuous grin as she demonstrated the leg lifts grated on Jessica's tense nerves. Breathing deeply, she stared at the television screen, her throat tight with the painful pressure of tears. Nothing was as easy as it looked. Not exercising. Not life. Her hands balled into obstinate fists. She would find Arthur another home. A *better* home.

Getting down on the carpet, Jessica began to do sit-ups. They were always easier when she was angry about something.

One and two and three and...

She would have to take a personal day off tomorrow and take Arthur back to the shelter. Maybe she could call the *Los Angeles Times*. Press coverage would definitely help.

Twelve and thirteen and...

Deliberately she painted cheerful mental pictures of being inundated with calls and letters from people wanting Arthur.

Twenty. No more.

Panting, Jessica lay down flat on her back. She closed her eyes and wished for a happy home for Arthur. And loneliness, blood pressure and anxiety for Dr. Karl Wagner.

Momentarily her heavy breathing stilled as she thought of Molly. The little girl was going to be terribly upset. Should she call and talk to her about Arthur?

No. That was Karl Wagner's problem. Let him handle it as best he could. She didn't want to be accused of interfering.

Promptly at eight the next morning, she stabbed the doorbell of Karl Wagner's house. Her face wore her ready-for-the-boxing-ring look. Arthur's deep woof welcomed her from the side of the house. Jessica's heart swelled with emotion at the thought of taking him back to the shelter even temporarily.

Karl Wagner answered the door quickly. Dressed in a navy pin-striped suit and a sparkling white shirt, he looked the epitome of success. His eyes held a watchful look. As if he expected her to spring at him and scratch his eyes out. As if he was the innocent party in all this. Jessica let out the air she'd been holding in her lungs and told herself all she had to do was stay calm for the next five minutes.

"I won't keep you," she said tersely, glad that anger had urged her toward a kelly green jumpsuit with an indigo-blue sash. She stuck out her chin, and the sunlight glinted off the saucerlike blue-and-green earrings she wore. "If you open the garage door, I'll get Arthur and be on my way."

"Come in for a moment." Karl's expression gave nothing away as he held the door wide.

Jessica thought she glimpsed a quirk at the corner of his mouth, but she was too angry to look again.

It was the first time she'd entered his house through the magnificent oak double doors. He led her past a blur of rooms, a curving staircase, into the family area she'd seen before.

The remains of his breakfast were on the dinette table, and he sat down as if she had all day to spare. "Would you like some coffee while I finish eating and then we can talk?"

"No, thank you." Jessica stood stiffly by the table. A quick look took in the glass of juice, the bowl of bran cereal. Feet slightly apart, she glared at him. "I don't have all day, so if you don't mind..."

"Arthur's what I want to talk to you about." Sounding the soul of reason, he poured a mug of coffee and placed it in front of her. "I'm not giving him up."

"What about...?" Jessica sank into the chair she'd been offered earlier. "Last night, last night..."

"I didn't say I was giving him away. *You* did."

"But I've taken the day off from work. I've called the Humane Society...." Words failed Jessica. She'd done it again. Jumped to conclusions. Staring at him miserably, the thought crossed her mind that the man was an inconsiderate boor. He could have called her back last night.

And you would have listened? He didn't even try. Hah!

"Cream? Sugar?" he asked. She helped herself to a spoonful of sugar with a hand that shook. Jessica lifted the mug to her lips and then set it down with a bang. She didn't want any of his coffee.

"What did you mean when you said last night that you wouldn't put up with any more of this?" A glacier was warmer than Jessica's tone. Her drop-dead look told its own story. She'd been saving that personal day off to spend with David at midterm.

"Just that. If you hadn't flown off the handle of your little broomstick and let me finish—" the now plainly visible quirk sent Jessica's blood pressure sky-high "—I would have explained that what I meant was that Arthur had to be trained not to dig holes."

"Oh." Jessica glared at him.

"When did you do this?" Her hand was imprisoned in his before she realized what he was doing.

"Do what?" Little tunnels of awareness pierced her anger, which Jessica refused to acknowledge.

"Get yourself a new set of nails."

"Oh, that." Jessica tried for cool, unwilling to admit the tunnels had fused into one great mass of emotion. There was no denying that she was tingling from head to toe.

"Yes, *that*."

Jessica cleared her throat as his eyes fixed on her face. The artificial, peach-colored nails weren't long or fancy, but they served their purpose. "Yesterday, during my lunch hour. It helped me stop biting them."

His thumb had found the ball of her hand again. Any more of that, and she would be reduced to the level of a harem slave. Eager, weak, *willing*.

Snatching her hand back, Jessica covered confusion with coldness. "If you're sure you want to keep Arthur, I might as well go in to work. Do you mind if I see him first?"

Karl nodded in the direction of the patio door. "Go ahead."

The reunion was brief. Jessica had eyes only for the yard. For the first time since yesterday, she acknowledged Karl's right to be furious. Arthur was a big dog and he'd dug big holes. Moon craters was an apt term. Looking at the yard, she understood how the holes had been filled. Underground sprinklers had turned each hole into a miniature lake. They were on now making the whole area look swampy. What little lawn was left was covered with overturned clods of grass and dirt. Jessica's heart sank.

Fixing a stern eye on Arthur, she lifted a finger and pointed to the holes. "Who did this?" she asked in the sternest voice she could muster. "Bad dog! You are *not* to dig any more holes." Jessica went over to one of the holes to make her point clear. *"No more holes."*

Arthur cowered, trying to shrink to half his size.

Jessica hardened her heart. For his own sake she had to get her point across. Picking up his nylon bone and a bright rubber ball Molly had mentioned buying him, she reiterated, "If you want to play, you play with these things. Digging holes is bad. No more holes."

Arthur gave a small woof. Jessica could almost swear he was laughing at her.

"You would certainly make a good trainer."

Karl was on the redwood deck, looking down at her. Smiling indulgently. *As if he liked what he saw. As if it mattered.* Dropping the bone and the ball, Jessica climbed the five wooden steps to the deck. It was time to leave.

Karl seemed in no hurry to be going anywhere.

"I won't keep you any longer," Jessica said as she wiped her damp palms down the sides of her jumpsuit. "Thank you for being so understanding about Arthur."

"You aren't keeping me. My first patient's at ten today. Feel free to continue training Arthur if you want to."

Jessica flushed as their gazes locked. Karl's seemed to be sending messages that puzzled Jessica. Confusion raged inside her. When had they made the transition from dog training to something as potent as this? Karl's gaze slid to her mouth. She wished he wouldn't keep doing that. It wasn't fair. It was also catching. Twice she'd had to tear her gaze away from his mouth.

Jessica's tongue flicked out to brush dry lips. "I'm sorry about your yard. It is an awful mess. You have every right to be angry." She wet her lips again and blinked. "Tell your gardener to send me the bill for redoing it."

Paying for it, even in installments, would probably take the rest of this life—and the next.

"It's not the money, Jessica. Forget what I said last night. I shouldn't have called you like that. It was just a shock on top of a long, rotten day. When I got back, Arthur wouldn't answer my call. I thought he'd run away again. I stepped off the deck to look for him and went calf-deep into a puddle."

The chuckle burst out of her spontaneously. Jessica covered her hand with her mouth. The thought of Karl's face when he stepped into a "moon crater" was too much to bear. Poor man. Had he been wearing a suit as expensive as the one he had on now? Imagining his trouser leg wrapped in wet mud, she began to laugh softly. He looked at her with one brow lifted, a whimsical smile tugging at his lips.

"I'm sorry." Jessica clung to the deck railing, giving full rein to humor. "I don't mean to be rude. It's just . . ." She doubled over again.

"I know." Karl's laugh mingled with hers. Warm, friendly, *healing*. "You should have seen my face. I got my leg out, took a step forward and there I was in another hole. For a few minutes I thought someone had dropped a bomb in my yard. Arthur stood by, wagging his tail. I swear he had a grin on his face. It took a while to realize he was claiming full responsibility.''

"Please . . . stop.'' Her sides ached as she put pictures to his words.

He watched her as if enjoying her laughter. Now and then he smiled ruefully. It was a while before Karl's gaze landed on her mouth, effectively cutting off all sound. Jessica's eyes shied away from the look on his face.

"What did you mean last night when you mentioned my mouth?'' The silky query ousted all thought, all control.

Her runaway tongue had done it again.

"Your mouth?'' She made her tone as vague as possible.

"You know what I'm talking about, Jessica. You said, quote, 'I must have been mistaken about your big heart, your kind mouth,' unquote. What did you mean?''

How many times had she vowed not to talk first, think later? She'd done it again. Got herself neck-deep in trouble.

Jessica stared at Molly's uncle, wondering how to convince him her opinion of his mouth was a purely clinical observation.

Chapter Four

"Jessica?"

There was no getting away from the truth. Not with Karl. He was waiting. Jessica had an idea he had the patience of a sphinx.

Reluctantly she turned to him. "Just that... just that mouths are an indication of a person's nature, and yours hints at kindness and generosity."

"I see." His expression gave nothing away.

"About your yard..." Every time she looked at it, something shrank inside. A mole would have envied Arthur.

Karl looked at her and smiled. It was a curiously intimate smile that shut out the rest of the world.

"Never mind fixing the yard." His voice was cotton-candy soft. One hand came up, and his knuckles skimmed her cheek as gently as a butterfly's caress.

Her legs shook so hard, Jessica could barely stand. Karl's touch singed her skin, making speech almost impossible. A drumroll of emotion had her pulse cavorting in a wild frenzy. She couldn't place the gleam in Karl's eyes, the softness around his mouth.

Jessica looked away. It was hard to keep her mind on track when her senses were derailed. "I'm truly sorry about the mess. It's just that Arthur's been through such a hard time lately. If you'd only give him a little time to get used to all this . . ."

The silence forced her to finally look up. The gleam was brighter, the intent expression in his eyes highlighting his pupils. Twin lasers of light leaped out and bound her as he said humorously, "With my mouth, do I have any other choice?"

Her gaze slid to his mouth, and for the life of her, Jessica couldn't look away.

She didn't resist when his hands took possession of her shoulders, or when his head blocked out the sky. In the one second his lips rested on hers, the world tilted on its axis. Her soul leaped out of her body to touch Karl's in midair. Time held its breath.

When she opened her eyes, Jessica blinked rapidly to bring the world back into focus. It was a good thing Karl had his arms wrapped about her, her face crushed to his chest. Her limbs weren't capable of supporting her just yet. Sensations strong as a tidal wave swamped that part of her brain that dealt with calm, cool, collected. Jessica's eyes closed again. Why fight anything that felt so good? This might be short, but she was going to enjoy the sweetness of every second. She concentrated on absorbing the feel of Karl, inhaling his personal scent, listening to his heart pound under her ear.

No one, Jessica acknowledged dreamily to herself, had mentioned a kiss could have so much power. Jessica slid her arms around Karl. His shirt felt soft and wonderful under her cheek.

The phone rang, startling her out of her dreamy state. Arthur barked, and Jessica blinked. What on earth had come over her? She tried to back out of Karl's embrace, but his arms tightened fractionally.

"Let it ring." His breath stirred her hair, sent a shiver down her spine.

"I . . . I should go to work." In her present state of mind, she would be lucky if she remembered how to drive. "We're working on a change of payroll. It always takes ages to sort out, and if I don't get in by eleven, my boss will put it down as half a day's vacation. . . ." She was babbling again. Jessica closed her mouth and stared at the puddles.

Karl lifted his head, stepped back. The quick glance she sent his way revealed that his wonderful mouth was turned up in one corner. Jessica's heart gave a responsive thump. There was a softness about Karl's smile she had never seen before.

"I really have to go." If she stayed, she would be lost.

Karl didn't even try to stop her. "Have a nice day," he called politely to her rapidly retreating back.

It was the kind of remark that strangers make to each other. Strangers that have nothing in common except a giant delinquent dog.

Molly called Jessica, Thursday night. "Uncle Karl's picking me up straight from school tomorrow afternoon. Can you come over Saturday morning to help me give Arthur a bath?"

He hadn't contacted her since Tuesday, proof that the kiss had been just a we're-both-curious-so-let's-get-it-over-with type of thing. Of course, the way she'd acted afterward wasn't exactly cover material for *Poise* magazine, either. She'd backed away from him and had been heading down the steps of the redwood deck when Karl had caught her arm. She'd looked up. Another kiss, and she wouldn't have had the use of her legs.

"The front door's this way, Jessica," he'd said kindly, turning her toward it.

She hadn't looked at him as she'd fled.

Now Molly wanted her to go back.

"Have you checked with your uncle about having me over?"

"I did," came the airy reply. "He said it was fine with him but I wasn't to monopolize all your time. He has to go to the clinic for a couple of hours. If you can come, I don't have to have a baby-sitter."

The patent disgust in Molly's voice at the idea of needing a baby-sitter made Jessica chuckle. If he wasn't there, going over to bathe Arthur could hardly be classified as chasing the man.

"I'll be there."

Defiantly Jessica looked at her reflection. Her closet had yielded long magenta shorts and a matching tank top. Over the outfit she wore an oversize emerald shirt. Massive green triangles dangled from her ears. She didn't care if it wasn't haute mode. It was the ideal dog-bathing outfit for a warm California day.

Karl had left a brand-new hose hooked up to a tap in the yard. To look at the yard now, no one would guess it had been redone only recently. Money and instant grass had worked wonders.

Molly hugged Jessica. Her smile was bright with affection. Jessica smiled back. She was becoming very attached to the eight-year-old. "Uncle Karl said we could bathe Arthur on the side patio."

Jessica followed Molly around the side of the house. The patio was covered with tiny gray-and-black rock embedded in concrete, shaped a perfect oval.

Molly pointed to the closed double doors. "That leads to the formal dining room. When Uncle Karl has parties, he opens the doors and people sit out here and look at the view."

It was certainly worth looking at. From this angle the snow-capped San Gabriel Mountains were plainly visible. At night the cities clustered at its foothills would sparkle like a diamond necklace.

"The last party Uncle Karl had here, I saw him kissing Maddy Brenton, his dentist friend." Molly giggled at the memory. "Mommy says though she wishes Uncle Karl would hurry up and get married, Maddy Brenton's not the right one for him."

Already Jessica found herself liking Karl's sister. She bent down to pat Arthur. There was no explanation for feeling winded. It was obvious Karl would have someone in his life.

"Jessica?"

"Hmm?" *Maddy Brenton*. Jessica rolled the words on her tongue. It was an awful name.

"How do you *know* the right person when they come along?" Molly looked extremely thoughtful.

"Well," Jessica said softly, her eyes on the gray-blue mountains in the distance. "When you meet someone you want to spend all your time with. When being away from that person makes you feel part of yourself is missing. When you look at him and know you don't want to change places with anyone else in the world. Then *that's* the right person for you."

"Oh!" Molly breathed. Jessica wondered what had prompted the girl's question. But a more urgent thought of her own pushed its own way in. Since when had she become an authority on the subject?

"Have you met anyone like that?" Molly's question was guileless. But with Karl's niece, that only cloaked deviousness.

"No, I haven't," she told Molly briskly, hoping her tone carried conviction. "Now, we've got a dog to bathe, remember? I don't think this is such a good spot. The patio's small, and we might get some water on the white double doors. Let's just go to the back and bathe Arthur by the deck. The shampoo and water won't hurt the grass. I read somewhere that soapy water aerates the soil."

And that ought to put ghosts of Maddy Brenton's kisses to rest.

Molly had bought enough shampoo for a dozen Great Danes. "I wasn't sure which kind to get, so Uncle Karl said to take one of each."

He would, thought Jessica grumpily as she put on Arthur's leash.

Money was no big deal, after all. Nor were people's feelings. How dare he kiss her just because he'd felt like it? It was time someone told him off.

"Watch the water, Molly." It had been a wise decision to wear her oldest clothes. The hose was being wielded with more enthusiasm than skill. Jessica watched Arthur lick Molly's face and the girl giggle happily. The Great Dane was definitely beginning to respond to Molly's love. Their developing rapport chased some of the chill away.

"How's your mother doing, Molly?" Cupping her palm, Jessica tilted the bottle and watched the golden liquid slide into her hand. The shampoo smelled good enough to use on her own hair.

"Better, but she has to stay in bed an awful lot. She had an ultrasound, and I saw a picture of the baby. We can't tell if it's a girl or a boy. Mommy and Dad don't want to know anyway, but I hope it's a sister.''

Jessica lathered Arthur's legs while Molly blew bubbles for him. The temperature had already climbed into the high seventies, but a light breeze tempered the heat. Two flowering pear trees provided a burst of bridal white on the slope. It was a beautiful day. A day for enjoying life.

Jessica determined to ignore the emptiness inside that longed for Karl's presence.

"Jessica, can I ask you something?"

"Sure." Gently she cleaned Arthur's face with the old washcloth Molly had brought out. With Karl's niece one had to be prepared for a discussion of anything from politics to dog ticks.

Molly set the hose down and looked straight at her. "Jessica, do people die from having babies?"

The sunshine seemed too bright all of a sudden. There was fear...and pain in Molly's voice. A heavy burden for an eight-year-old to carry around.

"These days," Jessica said gently, sitting down on her heels and taking Molly's hands in hers, soap suds and all, "very, very few people die having babies. Doctors are very careful. They have so many new ways of making sure mothers and babies are not in any kind of danger."

Molly's mouth wobbled. "I don't want anything to happen to my mommy."

Jessica wrapped her arms around the girl and held her close, her own eyes stinging. "Nothing will, honey, nothing will. She just has to stay in bed so she doesn't have the baby too soon, not because she's ill."

"Will the baby die if it comes too soon?"

Jessica swallowed. She couldn't make promises she couldn't guarantee. "Do you know that when I was born, I weighed four pounds? Twenty-three years ago doctors and nurses took such good care of me that I went home after a month. These days they have so many better ways of taking care of little babies, so much better equipment. I read somewhere that a mother had twins who weighed two pounds each, and they were both doing fine.''

Most of the worry left Molly's eyes. The rest, Jessica knew, would take time and the birth of the baby to remove.

Arthur helped restore things to normal by nudging Molly with his nose. They both looked at the patient Great Dane covered in lather and laughed.

''Let's get back to work before this stuff sticks to Arthur permanently,'' Jessica suggested.

With a giggle, Molly picked up the hose and started washing him off, while Jessica scrubbed the dog's coat with a soft nylon brush to make sure she got all the soap out. Molly, with a child's ability to switch moods, was telling Arthur he would smell like roses when this was all over. Deliberately Jessica encouraged Molly's excitement with stories of her own dog Trucker and his hatred for their unfortunate mailman.

Jessica wondered if she'd said the right thing to Molly. It was evident Molly didn't want to share her fears with her parents or her uncle. Worry was too big a burden for the child to bear alone. Maybe, thought Jessica, she should mention it to Karl when she saw him next. He might do a better job of reassuring his niece.

Buried in her thoughts, Jessica didn't see Karl on the deck or Arthur brace his legs to shake the excess water out. She was looking for the top of the shampoo bottle when the giant spray hit her. Backing away from it, she tripped on the hose and sat down hard. Molly giggled helplessly. ''Arthur got you, Jessica. Are you okay?''

When Jessica nodded, Molly continued mischievously, "You're soaked from top to bottom. A little more won't hurt."

Before Jessica could say a word, the nozzle was turned on her. Jessica gasped. The spray was gentle, but the first blast was cold.

"Stop that!"

They both turned to locate the source of the sound. The hose in Molly's hands swung around, too. Jessica's eyes closed in disbelief as a jet of water hit Karl's snow white shirt.

"Molly!" They both rapped out the name in unison.

"I'm sorry." The quickly dropped hose created a miniature pool around Jessica. She sat in the stream of water, wondering why she always looked her worst for him. Had her fairy godmother taken one look at her the day she was born, thrown her hands up in despair and resigned on the spot?

Karl ran down the steps and shut off the tap. Putting a hand out, he helped her to her feet. She was so wet, there was no explanation for the sparks that ignited wherever he touched her. Her hand, her back, literally burned. Jessica took her glasses off and blinked.

Molly picked up the old towel she'd brought out earlier and retreated with Arthur, keeping a wary eye on the grown-ups.

Tiny drops of water clung to Karl's dark hair, sparkling like crystals in the sunshine. The urge to reach up and touch them was overwhelming. The memory of the kiss returned full force, and with it, a blinding need to feel his mouth on hers again. Jessica looked around for something to wipe her glasses on.

"Are you all right?" Taking her glasses, Karl pulled his shirt out of his pants and wiped them with a corner of the soft white material. He inspected the lenses to make sure they were clean before setting the glasses back on her nose. "There you go."

Jessica flashed an anxious Molly a reassuring smile. "I'm fine. Arthur had me soaking wet already. I expected it, anyway—that's why I put on my oldest clothes. It's nothing a little while in the sunshine won't set right."

His gimlet look made her aware she was babbling again. There was something about him in the white shirt that had her heart imitating a calypso rhythm. It set off his tan to perfection, emphasized the impression of strength she'd absorbed at their first meeting. A pulse erupted in her throat as the memory of his lips on hers rose to taunt her. Jessica turned away to pick up the shampoo bottle. In her present condition there wasn't much left to the imagination. Holding the front of her top away from her body, she wrung out the excess water. A slight breeze made her break out in goose bumps.

Karl frowned. "You have to get out of these wet clothes or you're going to get chilled."

"I'm fine." Her teeth seemed inclined to chatter. Jessica clenched her jaw.

"You're not," he snapped. "Now, come with me. We can't have you getting sick. Molly, hit the upstairs shower."

Jessica stalked in front of him, seething. She hated domineering men. The kind that thought they knew what was best for you. The kind that were right. At the door of the patio, she stepped out of her waterlogged shoes and hesitated.

"Now what's wrong?" Karl asked with barely concealed impatience. "Are you going to give me another argument?"

"I don't want to drip water everywhere." It was sacrilege to step on the gleaming wooden floor or the silvery gray carpet beyond in her condition.

"It'll dry."

His tone indicated he didn't care what happened to the plush designer pile. Jessica hesitated. It was a shame to ruin the carpet. She had enough on her conscience as it was.

She tiptoed her way in. This way, at least the damage would be minimized.

She didn't want Karl to label her hazardous to his property. Every time they met, something got ruined. First his handkerchief, then his yard, now his shirt.

And since things couldn't get worse, they had to get better.

"Have a hot shower. You'll find plenty of towels in the small closet in the bathroom. I'll find you something to wear while your things dry."

"High-handed, bossy, imperious." Jessica compiled a list as the hot water beat blissfully down on her, chasing the incipient chill away. He was also right. If she'd stayed in those clothes, she would have caught a cold.

The eight-by-four glass-enclosed shower was hardly a cubicle. It was stocked with three kinds of shampoo, a fragrant creamy liquid soap that smelled out of this world and lathered like whipped cream.

Draping a thick, thirsty, ivory towel around her, Jessica peered out cautiously. There was a white toweling robe hanging on the doorknob. His. It was going to be miles too big.

Her breath left her body in a surprised whoosh as she slipped into the robe. The hemline and the sleeves had been butchered ruthlessly for her comfort. The jagged edges told her he had wreaked the damage with a pair of scissors. Jessica heart picked up the calypso rhythm again as she noticed the designer monogram. Was there no limit to this man's thoughtfulness? The next question was closer to home. Where could a levelheaded, self-sufficient woman buy herself some insurance against a man like Karl Wagner? She needed some very soon, very badly. Jessica pushed on her glasses and gathered her clothes with hands that shook.

The laundry room was directly opposite the bathroom. The door had been left ajar, so she didn't have to speculate on its location. After putting her things into the dryer, Jessica went out to the deck.

Karl turned at her approach and held out a mug of coffee. Jessica took it carefully and cupped her fingers around it, aware of his eyes on her, of a familiar churning in her stomach. He'd changed into a pair of cutoff shorts and a T-shirt. The breadth of his shoulders, the lean muscular legs with a smattering of dark hair, set her senses rioting. Pushing up her glasses, Jessica wondered how to break the tension. The frayed sleeve-length was her cue. She cleared her throat. "Why did you ruin your robe?"

"It's an old one." A half shrug dismissed further discussion of the subject. "Do you feel better now?"

"I'm fine."

He continued staring at her. Jessica knew she'd never looked worse. She hadn't used the hair dryer, because her hair tended to dry frizzy when she did. In spite of toweling it, it clung to her head like a wet mop. David called it her wet-rat look. Bare toes curled into the wooden deck as she raised her eyes to his. The queer flame was back, heralding his intentions. His gaze slid to her lips, and a fire ignited in the pit of her stomach. A hand came out and touched the tip of a wet lock of hair. Hypnotized, Jessica followed it as it moved to finger the lapel of her robe.

"Thank you for reassuring Molly about her mother's pregnancy."

"You heard?" Anxiously she looked at him. "Did I say the right thing?"

His hand wrapped around the side of her neck as his thumb flirted with her cheek. Jessica stood as still as a statue.

"You were perfect."

His eyes lingered on her mouth, and Jessica tensed in anticipation of the kiss. Her eyes closed of their own volition, and she rocked on her toes. She wasn't sure if this was correct behavior for a self-sufficient woman. She didn't care. She wanted to recapture the feelings that had accompanied their last kiss.

Instead of the heat of Karl's lips, she felt a blast of frigid air as his hand moved away from her neck. Jessica's eyes flew open.

"Karl?" He was four feet away, hands braced on the railing of the deck, gazing at the horizon as if special pictures were painted on it that only he could see.

He'd had no intention of kissing her.

Wave after wave of humiliation washed over her, each more hurtful than the last. Jessica opened her mouth to say something brilliant. Laugh the whole thing off. But the words wouldn't come. She couldn't even produce her usual croak. She looked down at herself. Embarrassment hadn't melted her to a puddle yet.

"I have to go in and check some paperwork."

Jessica would have accepted that if it hadn't been for the expression in Karl's eyes as he looked at her briefly. She identified it instantaneously. Confusion and control battled for supremacy. It was no small skirmish.

"Sure, go ahead," she said casually.

Her heart did a great big fillip of excitement as she watched him go in. Karl had *wanted* to kiss her. Though he hadn't, just knowing he'd wanted to, made everything all right. She hadn't been wrong. Lightning quick, her mind searched for reasons why he hadn't.

Maddy Brenton? Jessica's smile faded. Of course. Karl would never do anything dishonorable.

Moisture pricked her lids and was blinked away angrily. *Fool.* As usual she'd jumped to conclusions too soon. It must have just been the sun in Karl's eyes, and her imagination had done the rest. To even think he was fighting his attraction for her was a mistake.

"Jessica, are we going to train Arthur now?" Molly asked as she dashed out on the deck, wet patches on her clothes denoting a hastily dried body.

"In a little while, when my clothes dry," Jessica promised.

Molly ran off to talk to Arthur. Sinking into one of the deck chairs, Jessica wondered how she would get through the next hour. Her throat ached, and the beginnings of a headache nagged at her temples.

Molly looked up at her uncle as he came into the family room after loading their dinner dishes in the dishwasher. She was watching a cartoon video he'd rented for her earlier. Uncle Karl usually read the paper now. Molly depressed the pause button of the video control. This was as good a time as any to discuss what was on her mind.

"Uncle Karl?"

"Yes, Molly?" He looked at her and smiled.

"Have you met anyone you want to spend all your time with?"

"Anyone I…?" Karl frowned. Talking to Molly was like playing chess. One always had to think a few moves ahead.

Right now he couldn't see the reasoning behind her question. Maybe, he told himself, it was just a simple straightforward one. If it was, it would be a first.

"No, I haven't," he said cautiously.

"Have you met anyone who, when you're away from them, makes you feel as if part of you is missing?"

"No...." A memory of a sopping wet Jessica popped into his head out of nowhere. A smile that tugged at his heart. A mouth that begged to be kissed. Karl's frown intensified.

"Have you ever looked at anyone," continued his niece remorselessly, "and thought that you wanted to be with them forever? That you wouldn't change places with anyone in the world for a billion dollars?"

"Molly, what's this all about?" He glared at her.

Molly stared at the television screen thoughtfully. That was twice in one day she'd made Uncle Karl angry with her. "Oh, nothing. I was just wondering if you knew how to recognize love. Mommy says it would have to hit you on the head for you to know it."

There was no hint of a smile in his niece's eyes as she looked at him. Obviously his lack of ability in that area of his life didn't amuse her. "And what makes you think you're an authority on recognizing love?" Precocious was one thing. Infuriating, quite another.

"Not me, Uncle Karl," said Molly virtuously. "I don't know anything about it. Jessica told me those things."

After which, she went back to enjoying her movie. Uncle Karl, she noticed, turned a lot of pages, but he didn't seem to be doing any reading.

Karl had a suspicion his real answer for every question of his niece's had been in the affirmative.

For someone who never lied, he'd almost blotted his copybook tonight.

* * *

The telephone rang as Jessica unlocked the door to her apartment Monday night. She and Gina, a friend at work, had taken in a movie, something they did on a regular basis.

The telephone stopped as she set her bag down, and then it started again. Reminded of last week's call, Jessica grimaced and picked up the receiver gingerly.

"Jessica?"

"Hi, Karl!" She kept her voice cool. "Is something wrong?"

"It's Arthur..." he began.

Jessica couldn't keep the resignation out of her voice. "What's he done now?"

"It's nothing he's done. It's what he *isn't* doing that's bothering me. Jerry, the boy who walks him, called as soon as I got home to tell me yesterday's meal hadn't been touched. Today's hasn't, either. I even went out and got him some ice cream. According to Molly, he loves butter pecan, but he wouldn't even look at it. Do you think he's sick?"

"Maybe." Jessica's mind raced over the symptoms, checked them against her experiences with her two dogs. "Is he close by?"

"Yes." Karl must be out on the deck for the dog to be beside him. A picture of Karl leaning against the rail in a white shirt tantalized her, made concentration an effort.

"Touch his nose, will you, with the palm of your hand. Tell me if it feels hot and dry."

"It does," Karl said, sounding surprised. "What does that tell you?"

"He might be running a fever. Look, I'll call a vet and make an appointment for as soon as possible." It would be easier for her to do because she knew exactly what to say to the vet. Besides, some of them only took in small animals.

"They'll probably want to see him right away. Then, if you like, I can come over and give you a hand taking him in."

"Thanks, Jessica. I'd appreciate that."

The third vet she found listed in the Yellow Pages worked late and agreed to wait for them to bring in the Great Dane.

Halfway to Jacaranda Meadows, Jessica looked down and realized she'd pulled on a pink shirt with carmine flowers over blue pants. Jessica sighed. One of these days she would get it all right.

Right clothes, right man, right time.

Right man. Fear stabbed at her, altering her heartbeat. If that was the way her mind was working these days, she could be in real trouble. She was too familiar with her symptoms to ignore them. She'd seen four sisters and six brothers fall in love, get married. Change in dress, in attitude, were some of the first symptoms. Was she ready for that?

She had vowed that if loving someone meant being dominated, she didn't want any of it. Not that it mattered in this instance, she told herself immediately. Karl wasn't available even if she *was* interested.

Jessica glared at the stretch of freeway. It was ridiculous to build anything on a couple of kisses. Karl and she were like chalk and cheese. The *only* things they had in common were a hundred-and-thirty-five-pound dog and a little girl with an enormous intelligence quotient.

He hadn't reappeared Saturday. Not that she'd expected him to. Jessica had changed back into her clothes, convinced Molly to postpone Arthur's training session to next week and fled, all in record time. Molly had agreed to say goodbye for her and thank Karl for the loan of his robe.

Jessica glanced at it now. Laundered and neatly folded in a plastic bag, it reminded her of the crazy impulses he'd stirred in her that weekend. Never before had she experienced such a cacophony of sensation, such a wild desire to ask for more. Jessica clamped down on that particular train of thought. It was a road that led nowhere. Tonight would be strictly business. There must be no reruns.

Karl had the garage door raised and two powerful lights switched on as she pulled up in front of his house and parked by the curb.

"Thanks for coming over so quickly, Jessica."

The navy blue polo-neck top and faded blue jeans were molded to his frame. Her senses immediately rioted, overthrowing reason. Darn the man for looking like he did. This wasn't going to be easy.

"Arthur won't get into the Audi."

Karl had good cause to be worried. Lifting a hundred-and-thirty-five-pound dog into the car was out of the question.

Jessica opened both rear doors of the Audi. Slipping into the car on the left side, she patted the seat beside her and coaxed, "Come here, Arthur. Good boy, come here."

He came to her through the right rear door, laying his head dolefully in her lap. Jessica felt love well up in her. "What's the matter? Don't you feel well?"

His nose was raspy and his eyes dull. Jessica felt a finger of fear slide up her spine. She hoped it wasn't anything serious. Not now, when he and Molly had just found each other.

Karl didn't say anything during the ten-minute drive to the vet. Jessica began to wonder if he was upset. He had every right to be. His sleep interrupted, his yard ruined, his precious leisure time taken over. And this was just the beginning. What was it she'd told him at the Clearview Plaza? Arthur wouldn't be any trouble? Karl's anger had to be directed toward her, as well.

Arthur had evidently been to the vet on several previous occasions. Something about the smell of antiseptic must have revived memories, because he sat down in the doorway of the clinic and refused to budge.

"Come on, Arthur, good boy, come on."

All her coaxing didn't work. He pulled against her hold on the collar, and she couldn't do a thing. If he really decided to pit his strength against hers, he would be unmanageable.

"Arthur, come on, sweetheart." Rubbing his neck, she dropped her voice low. "We've got to get you better. Molly's going to be real upset if she hears you're sick. Come on."

She looked up at Karl, to find him watching her. Their gazes linked. Immediately a polite shield replaced the warmth in Karl's eyes. He was backing away from her again.

"Did he hurt your arm?" he asked. The question was cool and formal, but Jessica knew she wasn't mistaken about the flare of emotion she'd seen.

"No. He knows his own strength, I think. He just wants to make a point. He doesn't want to go in there."

Karl Wagner could teach the U.S. Army how to retreat.

She rubbed Arthur's head, then tried leading him in again. Pressing his forepaws into the ground, he flattened his ears. She couldn't budge him.

"If you could just push a bit . . . ?"

She would store up this memory and laugh about it later. Right now it took all hers and Karl's combined strength to get Arthur into the doctor's examining room. Both of them were breathing hard when Dr. Mills came into the room. One look at Arthur's size, and the vet said, "Relax, folks. I'm not going to ask you to lift him onto the examining table. If you'll wait outside, I'll be with you as soon as I examine your dog."

A girl appeared to help the vet as they returned to the waiting room.

Jessica tried to leaf through a magazine while they waited. It was hard to concentrate with Karl striding up and down. Every now and then she stole a glance at him. There was a leashed impatience about him, at odds with his usual calm. Twice he stopped and flung a glance her way as if he wanted to say something. Outwardly serene, Jessica flipped a page, staring blankly at a section that offered sixty-five recipes for ten-minute meals. The old man in the corner, clutching a Siamese kitten, watched them with avid curiosity. Evidently he'd picked up the tension between them and would love an argument to brighten his day. Jessica turned another page. Whatever Karl wanted to say had to wait till they got back to his place. She wasn't risking an argument here.

Jessica could almost guess what he would say. Arthur had to go back. She'd told Karl dogs lowered blood pressure, reduced anxiety. Somebody should have told Arthur that. So far he'd done everything possible to achieve exactly the opposite results.

"Well, folks, your dog's going to be fine." Jessica stood up as a beaming Dr. Mills came farther into the waiting room. "There's nothing seriously wrong with him. He's running a slight temperature, but as there are no other symptoms to go on, it might just be a chill. California weather's so strange at this time of year with a forty-degree temperature difference between night and day. Don't be in too much of a hurry to bathe him again, and make sure his bed's in a draft-free place. I've given him a shot, and here's a prescription for an antibiotic. Slip the tablets into a hot dog or wrap a slice of salami around it, and he'll take it. There's another way I'll show you later when he's more used to you. For now, this will do the trick. If he's not better in thirty-six hours, call me." Reaching out, Dr. Mills patted Jessica's shoulder kindly. "Not to worry, Mom."

It was a good thing Arthur was in as great a hurry to get back to the car as she was. Burying her face in the dog's side, she shook with laughter.

"Something wrong?" Karl peered at her.

Jessica lifted laughter-filled eyes to him. "I love Arthur," she said in a shaky voice, "but *Mom*?"

Karl looked at them sitting side by side on the back seat, threw back his head and roared with laughter.

A while later Jessica wiped her eyes. "A thought just occurred to me. If I'm Mom, do you know who Dr. Mills thinks *you* are?"

"Dad?"

They couldn't help the gales of laughter that followed. Arthur sensed their happiness and licked Jessica's hand approvingly as Karl, shoulders shaking, slid into the driver's seat.

"You know, he's beginning to get to me?" Karl's words broke the silence in the car when they were on the freeway. Jessica's jaw dropped. So the silence, the pacing had been worry...not impatience. "I was almost worried about him for a while there. Not just for Molly's sake. He's kind of grown on me, the way he waits for me to come home. I barely say a word to him, and yet seeing me seems to make him wildly happy. He sits by the patio door as long as I'm in the family room, even if I close the drapes. I don't do anything for him."

In the darkness Jessica smiled her Mona Lisa smile. Arthur's own special brand of charm was beginning to work. She'd counted on that. She wasn't aware of the huge sigh of relief that escaped her. Happy endings were wonderful.

"Tired?" The warmth was back in Karl's voice.

"Not really." Jessica frowned, trying to figure the man out.

He thinks he's safe in the darkness, that I won't see anything he doesn't want me to.

"Thanks for coming over so quickly."

"It's nothing," she said. "I meant what I said that day in the mall about helping you with him. I'm just sorry Arthur's disrupting your life so much."

"No one can help being sick."

There was nothing to say in light of such reasoning. Jessica stared out at the darkness quietly.

Why was Karl denying his feelings? The more evidence he gave her that he was, the more Jessica wanted to solve the puzzle Karl's behavior presented.

Chapter Five

Urging a sleepy Arthur out of the car and onto his piece of carpeting in the garage took no time at all. Jessica noted the new dog door cut into the side of the garage gave Arthur access to it.

"I guess that's all we can do for him now. He'll be fine. I'd better be going." Keeping her voice light, Jessica checked his water dish before giving Arthur one last loving pat. She couldn't express the urge that came over her to stay a while longer.

"Have you eaten?" Karl asked. Jessica looked up to see him holding the door into the house open for her.

"Not yet." Suddenly her feet dragged. Her emotions were on a seesaw. One minute she wanted to stay, get to know Karl better. The next, she wanted to put as much distance as she could between this man and herself. "I have something I can warm up at home."

"Do you like Chinese food? I brought home some take-out today." When had Karl decided she was staying? For the umpteenth time, Jessica told herself she disliked men who made up her mind for her.

"I don't want to deprive you of your dinner," Jessica protested, wondering why she couldn't be firmer about leaving.

"You won't. I brought plenty. Come on in."

The door from the garage opened directly into the laundry room Jessica had seen on her last visit. In the family room Karl invited her to sit down and switched on the evening news. Jessica balanced on the edge of a black leather couch as Karl washed his hands and began emptying the contents of the white take-out cartons into dishes. He moved around the kitchen, heating food in the microwave, setting the table for two, with the ease of someone used to doing things for himself.

Jessica looked around, appreciating again the modern plan of Karl's home that had the family room in plain view of the kitchen and vice versa.

It would be easy to watch kids playing here while one worked in the kitchen.

Her breath stuck in her throat. Why on earth was she thinking of children and watching them? Her heartbeat accelerated. All at once Jessica was very conscious of being alone with Karl. Of needs and impulses that surged blindly to the top. Nervously she pushed up her glasses.

Watching the news while they ate filled in the gaps in their conversation. The chow mein and sweet-and-sour chicken that she normally would have enjoyed tasted like blotting paper. The eating island in the kitchen seemed like a small oasis shutting them off from the rest of the world. She could feel the warmth from Karl's body as she sat next to him. He'd jostled the two chairs closer on the side that faced the television. His presence shut off sanity. To Jessica's keyed-up senses, every second seemed to slow down.

Afterward Jessica insisted on loading the used dishes in the dishwasher as Karl put things away in the refrigerator and wiped the table. It was time to call it a day. Tiredness always aided her overactive imagination, which certainly didn't need any help.

Jessica was caught openmouthed when Karl turned to her and suggested, "Let's go into the other room for a while, shall we?" Becoming aware of her expression, he lifted his mouth in its familiar quirk. "You were about to say?"

"I can't remember." Jessica blinked.

What other room? she wondered wildly as she followed him. Reminded of the suddenness with which he'd kissed her, the level of weakness he always reduced her to, Jessica felt her nerves begin to jangle.

Karl led her through a hallway. Suddenly they were in a marble entryway the size of her apartment. Jessica vaguely remembered walking through it before. Anger hadn't let her observe details on that occasion. Now she took everything in.

The sunken living room looked as if it belonged on the sets of *Dynasty*. An enormous white cathedral ceiling sloped upward. Jessica's gaze was caught and held by the tiny glitters embedded in the nubbly texture of the ceiling.

Now why, she wondered, would anyone put sparkles up there? I mean, there's no way one could see them or appreciate them unless, unless...

The thought of the position one would have to be in to appreciate that particular aspect of Karl's home, its accompanying suggestiveness, vacuumed the breath from her lungs. Jessica threw a blanket over her overactive imagination and looked around.

The room was an awe-inspiring ocean of chrome and glass. Huge glossy plants broke up the severity. On one wall was an enormous painting Jessica thought she might understand better if she stood on her head to look at it.

She hesitated, almost afraid to step down.

"We could just use the family room," she began hesitantly.

Karl looked up from where he knelt in front of the fireplace. There was no doubting his surprise at her suggestion. "Why?"

"I don't know. This room's so...so...elegant."

Maddy Brenton would fit in here perfectly.

He frowned, then said, "Don't be silly, Jessica."

Moving the brass screen in front of the fireplace aside, he set a match to the single log there. The sharp short jabs with which he pushed the buttons on an elaborate stereo system told Jessica he was annoyed. Gentle classical music, at odds with the tension in the room, filtered through hidden speakers. Sitting down gingerly on the very edge of one of the pale peach couches, she studied the glass figure of a woman, head thrown back, arms raised to the skies. She'd seen something like it recently in a magazine. If her memory served her right, it cost close to two months of her salary. Jessica tightened her spine. This was definitely not a room one relaxed in.

Apparently Karl didn't think so. Sweeping the black-and-peach cushions off the other couch, he arranged them on the floor.

Jessica blinked. Her imagination hinted at romance in the air. She threw another blanket over it.

"Would you like some wine?"

"No, thank you." A sudden surge of adrenaline made her hands damp and interfered with her breathing.

Something in her tone made Karl turn from his contemplation of the fire. A frown creased his brow. "Why on earth are you perched on the edge like that?" he asked.

"Here, take your shoes off, sprawl if you want to. Make yourself comfortable while I get some wine."

Jessica looked at the sheen of the silver carpet. No, she didn't think it would forgive sprawling. She did move back a couple of inches, though. It was either that or fall off the edge.

Karl returned with two wine glasses and an unopened bottle, saying, "I got you some juice."

"Th-thank you." Jessica wet her lips. She had some explaining to do. The sooner she got it over with, the better.

Karl turned to her. The look in his narrowed eyes slashed its way to her soul. Jessica shrank and stared at the fire. What she had to say couldn't wait any longer.

"I . . . It's all my fault that Arthur's sick." The confession made her feel worse, not better. She should have been more careful.

Karl's eyebrows rose. "What makes you say that, Jessica?"

"I . . . I shouldn't have bathed Arthur. You heard what the vet said about not being in too much of a hurry to bathe him again. Earlier, on the telephone he told me Arthur's coat should be brushed daily and cleaned once in a while with pads saturated in rubbing alcohol."

The flickering flames reminded Karl of the way her mouth had felt under his. Gentle, exploring, *inexperienced*. Compunction pierced him as he listened to her apology and teamed with a protective gentleness.

"It's not your fault he's sick, Jessica," he said calmly. "Bathing Arthur was Molly's idea. *I* should have looked it up in the dog book, but I didn't think it would hurt to bathe him. So, if you have to blame someone, blame me."

"I've always bathed my own dogs," she said as she twisted a tissue in her hands and stared down at it. "I've never heard about cleaning a dog any other way till today."

Karl sat down on the carpet, propping himself against the couch. "Tell me about your family, Jessica."

She almost dropped her glass. Head tilted, she thought of his words. Imagination insisted he'd just said something about returning Arthur to the shelter. But he hadn't. Her tension had obliterated the first part; she'd definitely caught the last words. *Your family.*

Jessica tried to marshal her scrambling senses, summon pictures of her family. "Mom and Dad live in San Francisco. They have a home-supply store in Oakland."

"Do you have any brothers or sisters?"

"Six brothers, four sisters."

He turned toward her, surprised. "A really large family."

Jessica nodded. The ice was melting. Thoughts of her family always warmed her. "Yes. My mother's decision to have a large family wasn't based on religious reasons or anything like that. She taught nursery school before she married my dad and just loves children. She always says her family is her only wealth."

"Do you want a large family, Jessica?" It seemed important to know.

"I'm not sure. It would depend on so many things. The man I marry, our financial circumstances, the size of family he wants. I think I'd like four children."

"What was it like growing up in such a big family?"

The love and friendship Jessica associated with her family showed in her voice when she spoke. "It was fun. I was never lonely or bored. I'm the youngest girl. When you're at the tail end, you also have very little chances of growing up spoiled. I didn't like having so many people telling me what to do. I remember my mother putting up a duty list each week that we kids had to follow. We were all very self-reliant and responsible." Jessica's eyes glowed with her rec-

ollections. "With so many of us, the adventures we had as
a family made television seem boring."

"What made you decide to move to southern California?"

Seriousness threw a shadow on her face as she answered
him, barely aware that she'd slid off the couch and was sitting on a cushion next to him. "Large families also mean
patterns being set by the older children that the younger
ones automatically follow." Marriage, settling down with a
good man, was the pattern four sisters had set. All had
married men like her father. Very much the head of the
family. Jessica wasn't ready to follow in their footsteps. She
could never be happy in the role of "little woman." Marriage, to her, was a partnership, not an autocracy. "Sometimes being part of a large family means being
overprotected. I had to get away, find out who Jessica
Hansen really is, see if she could survive on her own, before it was too late."

"And . . . ?" Karl prompted.

"And I've found I like living on my own, making my own
decisions, taking care of myself." Jessica sipped the juice,
wishing she'd asked for wine.

"You've established your individuality, haven't you?"

"Yes." She didn't want to mention she intended to keep
things this way for the rest of her life. She didn't want to be
dominated ever again. If she couldn't find a man who
thought the same way, she preferred to remain single.

Karl stared into the fire. He guessed it had been no small
battle for her. Her size invited protectiveness, the auto-
matic idea that she needed taking care of. But one only had
to talk to her to know that was the last thing Jessica needed.
She could take care of herself.

Was he bored? Jessica wondered what Maddy Brenton would have talked about. Dental innovations, nuclear warfare, world peace?

"Karl, tell me about your family."

He looked at her, and for a minute Jessica was thrown by the veil of bitterness in his eyes. A sore spot?

"I grew up in Grosse Pointe, Detroit. There was just my sister, Andy, and myself. Parochial schools, Stanford, and then I decided to come and start a practice here."

Jessica could almost see the curtain that had come down between them. It was cold, too, as if Karl had drifted away from the warmth of the fire into the icy clutches of his past. His short, bald sentences told her more than any speech would have. There was an emptiness within him that didn't want analysis.

Growing up in a large family had provided each of the Hansen children with the experience and insight it took a psychologist years to gather. It was time to change the subject.

Jessica leaned back against the cushions. "Why did you decide to become a dentist?"

Karl's face changed, lightened. "Once, when I was about nine, I broke a tooth. My mother took me to the dentist. I was terrified because I'd always associated dentists with pain and fear, though I'd never been to one. My mother went often, and she was always tied up in knots the whole week she went. That fear communicated itself to both Andy and me. I was scared sick of going to the dentist. My mother took me to Dr. Hayes, who specialized in children's dentistry." Karl's face softened with the memories. "The man was wonderful. He talked to me and explained exactly what he was going to do. He told me that except for the first prick of the needle, if he caused me any pain, he would let me kick his shin for every twinge I felt. I was so busy waiting for the pain, I didn't remember any of the treatment. When it was over, he lifted the leg of his pants and said, 'Well young man, how many times?' I couldn't say a word, just shook my head. I hadn't felt a thing."

Karl took a sip of his drink, smiled and then continued. "'You keep this a secret between us,' Dr. Hayes said, shaking my hand, his eyes full of humor. 'If you go out and tell everyone how much fun this was, I'm going to have so many patients I won't be able to go home to my wife and kids.' Twenty-one years ago there weren't many dentists like him. I looked at Dr. Hayes and knew I wanted to be exactly like him. Have the tremendous power of replacing fear and pain with confidence and courage."

It was Jessica's turn to be silent. Beneath that slightly cool exterior Karl showed the world lay enough warmth to melt the North Pole. She blinked rapidly as she pushed up her glasses with one hand.

Emotion so thick she could almost touch it swirled between them. Jessica wanted to reach out and put her arms around Karl, press her lips against his.

Only the fear the gesture might constitute an attack in her personal book of proper behavior held Jessica back. It wasn't easy, living with an overdeveloped conscience.

"I have to go now." It was ten-thirty. Chances were she wouldn't be able to fall asleep. Chances were she wouldn't be able to wake up on time tomorrow.

Karl got to his feet in one swift movement, held a hand out to her. Jessica put her hand in his and was pulled up to within an inch of his chest.

"Thanks for coming over."

"Don't even mention it," she ordered gently. "Call me anytime you need help with Arthur."

His eyes moved to her mouth. "Feeling better now?"

"Feeling better?" she echoed. Karl's question didn't make sense.

"You were so tense when we came in here." His expression revealed he'd been privy to her thoughts. That he'd cared enough to restore her peace of mind made Jessica want to cry.

She nodded.

Karl searched her face and said, "There's one thing I have to clear up. Arthur's our responsbility now. Every time something happens I don't want you blaming yourself for it. I don't hold anything he does against you. Time passes so quickly on the weekends now. I don't have to worry about entertaining Molly. Arthur makes a splendid companion, and she loves caring for him. So, no more punishing yourself, all right?"

Jessica swallowed hard. Did Karl know he was a genius at eradicating fear outside his dental clinic as well as in it? She nodded again. There weren't any right words for the way she felt.

Karl placed a warm hand on the small of her back and steered her to the door.

"Drive carefully."

She tried to say something casual, brilliant, unforgettable. What came out was a croak. "Good night."

In the five minutes it took to reach her apartment, Jessica tried to put all the pieces of Karl Wagner together. One part of her puzzle was still missing. Why had Karl decided to put his personal feelings on hold indefinitely? Why was he denying himself the most important kind of love? He had that special knack of catering to everyone else's inner needs. Would he ever let anyone cater to his?

* * *

He called her again Friday night.

"How is Arthur?" *Please don't say Arthur's causing more trouble.*

"He's much better," Karl reassured her immediately. "He's eating again, and I haven't had any trouble giving him his medicine. It's Molly I wanted to talk about, if you have the time."

"Go ahead. I'm not doing anything important." Jessica unbuckled the belt of her dress and sank onto the couch, one leg curled up under her.

"Andy's worried about her. Molly's been kind of withdrawn all week, doesn't want to talk much to either her mom or her dad. Just stays in her room most of the time and says she wants to work on her stamp collection. But all she really does is lie on her bed and stare at the ceiling. Yesterday was Valentine's Day, and Jim and Andy had planned a special catered dinner as a treat for Molly, but she barely ate anything. As soon as dinner was over, she excused herself and went to bed. That isn't like her. Nothing unusual's happened this week, so Andy just can't figure out the reason behind the withdrawal. We were wondering if she said anything to you that would clue us in."

"Nothing really." Jessica searched her memory bank for anything that might help Molly's parents and came up blank. This didn't seem the right time to thank him for the red and white carnations she'd received yesterday. The accompanying card had read, "With love from Molly, Arthur and K.W." It was unexpected...and very confusing. He didn't seem the type who went in for casual messages.

"The worry's not good for Andy. The thought that something's wrong and Molly won't tell her *because* of Andy's state of health is doing more damage than her condition itself."

"It would," agreed Jessica. Suddenly it was of paramount importance to remove the cloak of worry from Karl's shoulders. "Maybe tomorrow I can spend some time with Molly and see if she talks to me about it."

"We could go to the beach with Arthur," he suggested, the worry still showing in his tone. "Molly loves the ocean."

"That sounds great. And Karl?"

"Yes?"

"Let Molly call me herself and invite me, okay? That way she won't feel she's being set up." Smart as Molly was, she would pick up the slightest hint and know what was going on. It might make her withdraw from them, as well.

"Sure. Thanks, Jessica."

Jessica replaced the receiver and went into her bedroom to think.

Molly called at eight, Saturday morning. "Jessica, did I wake you up?"

"Yes." Jessica opened one eye, waited for the world to come into focus.

"I'm sorry. Shall I call you back?" Molly asked politely, though the excitement threaded through her tone came across clearly.

"No. That's all right."

"Jessica, Uncle Karl said we could take Arthur to the beach today. Would you like to come with us?"

Adrenaline pumped through her, driving the last vestige of sleep away. "The beach." Her mind went blank for a microsecond, then pictures rushed in. Karl in swimming trunks, Karl in the ocean. "Let me think a minute."

"Uncle Karl's taking a picnic lunch, and Arthur wants to go," coaxed Molly.

"Who else is coming?" Jessica asked, not wanting Molly to realize she knew all about the plan.

"No one," Molly said, sounding surprised. "Just Uncle Karl and Arthur and me and you if you want to come."

"Yes," she told Molly as she threw back the covers and stood up, full of energy. "Yes, I do. What time are we going to leave?"

"Well, Uncle Karl has to go to his clinic at ten. He said if you wanted to drive over there with Arthur and me at eleven-thirty, we'd go then."

"Who's going to watch you from ten on?"

"I have to stay with the baby-sitter." The insult in Molly's tone widened Jessica's smile.

"Not if I'm there by ten, right?" Jessica said.

"Would you, Jessica? Thanks! I'm not supposed to ask you, but if you offer, that's different." Molly was clearly pleased by the turn of events. "If you're a few minutes late, it's okay. Mommy told Uncle Karl I can be left alone for half an hour, not longer."

"See you at ten, or a little after," Jessica said, then put the phone down and rushed to the bathroom. A picture of Molly a few years from now in the Pentagon, organizing defense strategies came to mind.

Karl had already left when she got there. Molly opened the front door, Arthur close at her heels.

"Is he allowed in the house?" Jessica thought of the fragile, expensive things in the living room. Arthur had no idea he wasn't a ballet dancer.

"Yes." Molly nodded. "I didn't even have to ask. When Dad brought me over last night, Arthur was in the family room with Uncle Karl. Uncle Karl said Arthur keeps him company in the evenings now. Arthur sits with his face on Uncle Karl's feet while he watches TV."

Jessica blinked as she imagined Arthur and Karl together. The next instant, something else Molly had said surfaced. *Keeps him company.* Where on earth was Maddy

Brenton? Jessica's heart gave a loud cheer. Absent was as good as unimportant.

"Molly, thank you for the nice flowers you sent me on Valentine's Day."

A secretive look crossed Molly's face. She said carefully, "They're from Uncle Karl and Arthur, too."

Jessica nodded. "I know, and they're really pretty."

"I'm glad you liked them." Jessica couldn't put her finger on the reason for Molly's uneasiness, but experience with a horde of nephews and nieces told her the eight-year-old was up to something.

"Uncle Karl says when we go over to his clinic, we can let Arthur out of the car." It was obvious Molly wanted to change the subject. "At the side of the building there's a part he had fenced in last week. A kind of dog run. He said it might be too hot in the car for Arthur and he'd be more comfortable outside. Sometimes Uncle Karl gets held up with a patient."

A dog run beside his clinic. Now, why would he have one there?

"How's your mother doing?" Jessica asked casually.

They were in the kitchen. Arthur flopped down by the couch with a huge sigh, apparently worn out by the exertion of greeting her.

A flash of worry clouded Molly's brow. "She's feeling better, but she still has to be careful."

"She's going to be fine." Jessica put every ounce of confidence into her tone. "I bet you're looking forward to having a baby in the house."

"Not really." Molly's bottom lip quivered. "Not if the baby's going to make Mommy so sick."

Thin ice. Jessica put an arm around the girl's thin shoulders and gave her a hug. "You'll change your mind when you see the baby. It's not really the baby that's making your mommy sick. It's her body that's made that way. You told me once she lost another baby, remember? Well, I think your mommy knew this wasn't going to be easy, but she still wanted to go ahead and have another baby.''

"Why?" demanded Molly. "She has me."

"Sometimes," said Jessica slowly, "when parents enjoy one baby very much, they want to go through the experience again. That's why my parents had such a large family. Sometimes they feel they want their child to have company so that it won't grow up alone. There are so many different reasons. Why don't you talk to your mommy about it?"

"Do you think it's going to upset her if I ask her these things?"

Jessica hugged the girl tightly. "Molly, I don't think anything you ask her is going to upset her. My mother always says when we're talking to her, even if we're arguing, she knows everything is going as it should. It's when we're quiet she gets worried. And mothers don't deserve the silent treatment."

While Molly thought it over, Jessica opened the back door to let Arthur out for a bit before they left for the clinic.

"I have to change his water." Molly streaked past.

Jessica watched them in the yard. Molly was going to be fine. She wished it was as easy to solve her own problems as it was to solve other people's.

Jessica shifted in the blue chair uncomfortably. She should have worn something else. The canary yellow beach pants and matching tank top covered with a loose mandarin orange shirt weren't the right things for the waiting room of Karl's clinic.

She looked around at the tastefully done walls in amethyst and mocha. Half of the room was a huge play area, complete with little playhouse and furniture. Everywhere there were things calculated to tempt a child to play, explore, experience. This wasn't a waiting room in the tense, drawn out, tortured sense of the word. It was a place guaranteed to divert even the most nervous child. One tiny tot was occupied with a book. Molly sat on a chair shaped like a giant tooth, coloring a picture.

Mrs. Lucas had smiled warmly at them as soon as they'd come in. Jessica had taken one look at the receptionist and been reminded of her grandmother. Someone a person could discuss anything with, from the state of one's health to a recipe for apple pie.

"Hi, Mrs. Lucas," Molly had greeted. "Come and take a look at Arthur."

"Jessica, how are you?" Karl said, appearing behind Mrs. Lucas, looking devastatingly handsome in a white coat. "I won't be long."

Aware she was staring at him, that Mrs. Lucas was watching them both, Jessica gathered her scattered senses and nodded. Karl picked up a file and disappeared.

"Are you coming?" Molly asked Mrs. Lucas again.

Mrs. Lucas hurried out from behind the glass partition, her face wreathed in smiles. "Oh, my! Is he here to visit us again? I have to see if he remembers me from yesterday. He's such a good dog."

"You haven't met Jessica yet," Molly reminded.

"I know Miss Hansen." Mrs. Lucas smiled warmly at her again. Jessica had an idea the receptionist would never be short of smiles. "We spoke on the phone some time back."

Formalities taken care of, Molly reverted to the subject dear to her heart. "Do you like my dog?"

"When Dr. Wagner brought him in on Tuesday, I almost refused to have anything to do with him, he's so huge. Dr. Wagner tied him up and filled his dishes. I went out later to see if he was okay and he just looked at me out of those big brown eyes of his, and I was lost. He's such a lamb."

"Why did Uncle Karl bring him to work Tuesday?" demanded Molly. "To show the kids?"

"No," trilled Mrs. Lucas. "Arthur wasn't feeling so good, and Dr. Wagner, bless his kind heart, didn't want to leave him home alone. Said he hates being alone when *he's* sick and it can't be much different for anyone else. Between patients he'd talk to Arthur out of his office window."

Jessica's mouth went slack. She pushed up her glasses. Karl had brought Arthur to work with him? The man may not know it, but he'd just signed up as a dog lover.

He hates to be alone when he's ill. Said it can't be much different for anyone else.

Jessica swallowed. How did one measure sensitivity, caring that went beyond the call of normal kindness?

Arthur stood up at their approach, tail wagging nineteen swipes to the dozen. When Mrs. Lucas put her hand out, he licked it. The office manager's smile threatened to split her chubby face in two.

"And how's my boy today, huh? All better?" She tickled him under the chin. "There's a good fella."

Jessica and Molly fought to keep a straight face. Mrs. Lucas's tone as she crooned sweet nothings to Arthur was a sharp contrast to her normal, brisk one.

Mrs. Lucas looked at them and said, "I had to call all over town Tuesday for someone to come and put up the chain-link fence right away. Dr. Wagner didn't want Arthur tethered all day. He said the dog needed his freedom. It's good to see him with an animal. They slink past your guard better than humans can."

Jessica could tell Mrs. Lucas referred to the same curtain of reticence in Karl that she was puzzling over. She shot the older woman a look as Molly ran to the end of the dog run with Arthur. Had Mrs. Lucas sensed Jessica *wanted* to remove that particular partition? The older woman's expression gave nothing away.

"Well, I guess I'd better go in." The older woman gave Arthur one last pat. "Dr. Wagner asked me to let you know he's going to be another half hour or so. One of his patients had an emergency, and I've never known him to refuse to see anyone. Works much too hard and then gives his money away as if it was water. I can't tell you how many people he treats free. Other dentists train their staff so that one of the first questions is 'Do you have insurance?' Dr. Wagner keeps reminding us if his first priority is money, he doesn't deserve to be called *doctor*." Jessica blinked as Molly rejoined them, and Mrs. Lucas said briskly, "He said if you both want to go shopping or anything, he'll wait for you here."

Jessica and Molly looked at each other. Molly shook her head and said, "I'd rather wait in the office if that's all right with you, Jessica. Uncle Karl's got some new coloring books. I'm going to do a picture for my mommy."

"I'll wait, too." She needed some quiet time to sort out her thoughts.

For the past ten minutes, Molly had been occupied with the things in the play area. Jessica flipped through a magazine briefly, then put it down. She shifted in her seat again and caught the eye of a patient's mother waiting in the room.

"Dr. Wagner's marvelous with children," the woman said with a hesitant smile. "There's absolutely nothing to be nervous about."

Jessica opened her mouth and closed it again. The woman thought she was nervous for Molly's sake?

"Your little girl will be just fine," Jessica's sympathizer continued. "When I brought Summer here, I didn't know what to expect. We'd neglected dental hygiene, thinking she was only a baby. By the time she was three and a half, she had seventeen cavities, and our dentist recommended we take her to a pedodontist, a children's dentist. He suggested Dr. Wagner, said he was the best in the area. I was scared stiff when I came here the first time. Dr. Wagner spent as much time with me as he did with Summer that visit, reassuring me, explaining her treatment. As for Summer, by the time her first filling was done, she would have done anything for him."

The young mother laughed, but Jessica could see the shimmer of tears in her eyes as the woman continued. "She thinks coming to Dr. Wagner is a treat. We had a hard time today, explaining to her that she wasn't going to see him today, that it was her cousin Berry who had the toothache. My sister, Berry's mother, works on Saturdays, so I offered to bring him in. Well, Summer started yelling her head off when the nurse came out for Berry. Dr. Wagner came out, took one look at her face and told her she could come in and pick out a toy, anyway, because she was a special friend. Every child gets to pick out a toy from a large box he has inside, before their treatment. He's a wonderful human being, not just a great dentist."

Jessica swallowed hard. She couldn't trust herself to speak.

Summer's mother blew her nose. "Wish I'd had someone like him when I was growing up."

"Like who?" said the flaxen-haired child who had been looking at a book. "Like who, Mom?"

"Like Dr. Wagner, Summer."

The four year old scrambled onto a chair beside her mother. "He's *my* dentist," she announced importantly. A pause while Jessica watched the child's forehead wrinkle in thought. Her next words came out on a sigh. "But sometimes I have to share him with other people."

The door opened to let out a grinning six-year-old. The wad of gauze in his mouth didn't detract from his cheeky smile.

"Dr. Wagner had to take out my tooth, but he said the tooth fairy would come, anyway, if I keep my tooth under my pillow tonight." The triumphant announcement earned him a sour glance from his cousin.

As the mother went to the window, checkbook in hand, Jessica watched Summer glare at her cousin. There were tears in the little girl's eyes. Summer opened her mouth, shut it, shook her head. Finally she tried again. "Dr. Wagner's *my* dentist," she hissed, checking to see her mother was out of hearing range. "I'm going to marry him when I grow up 'n never let him work on *your* teeth, so there!"

Chapter Six

It was a balmy eighty degrees at the beach. Molly ran to the water's edge soon after they got there, Arthur on a leash beside her. Already a few children had gathered around to stare at the Great Dane. Jessica watched as Molly stopped and the children came closer to ask about Arthur. Molly's voice carried clearly to where Karl and Jessica sat, as she began, "Once upon a time Arthur belonged to another family..."

"No sign of withdrawn now." They shared a smile before Karl returned to his inspection of the picnic basket. "I can't wait to see what Mrs. Lucas's cousin has in here." Catching sight of the surprise on Jessica's face he said, "Didn't I tell you, Edna's cousin runs a catering business? He fixes picnic baskets for me through the summer and caters complete dinners when I entertain." Jessica flinched as she thought of how special his last party had been. Maddy Brenton, kisses and all. "Ah, my favorite. Fried chicken and mashed potatoes. Want to try some now?"

"No, thanks."

Karl picked up a leg and bit into it. "Just making sure they did a good job." His lighthearted smile revealed a rare glimpse of the boy in him. He seemed relaxed and happy. Evidently Molly and Karl both loved the beach.

Jessica sat on the blanket Molly had helped her spread and watched Karl. It was becoming her favorite pastime.

After the last patient had left Karl's office earlier, Mrs. Lucas and two assistants had bustled out.

"Dr. Wagner's changing his clothes," Mrs. Lucas had told Jessica and Molly on her way out. "He'll be with you in a minute."

The cut-off denim shorts and T-shirt that Karl had come out in five minutes later emphasized the width of his shoulders and interfered with Jessica's breathing.

They had decided to leave her car in front of the clinic. Karl would drop her back there at the end of the day.

"Want a drink?" he asked now, the muscles bunching under his shirt as he held one out to her.

"Thanks." Jessica took the soft-drink can and wrapped both hands around it. Her imagination had rushed off on a different track.

How many romantic dinners à deux had Mrs. Lucas' cousin catered for Karl? she wondered. A picture of him and Maddy Brenton holding hands by candlelight made it hard to swallow.

"You're awfully quiet," Karl said, glancing at her again. "Is something wrong?"

"No."

There was so much to think about. All the pictures she'd gathered of Karl that morning added up to warm, wonderful, kindhearted. Why was he denying himself a warmer, closer relationship?

"Did Molly talk to you this morning?"

"Yes," Jessica said, nodding. At least this was one area where she could help Karl. "Molly's beginning to resent the baby, blame it for what her mother's going through. We discussed it, and Molly said she's going to talk to your sister about it."

"You're sure it's nothing more than that?"

"Yes."

"Thank goodness."

Jessica was surprised by the vehemence in Karl's tone. Surely he knew Molly's fears were natural?

Karl lifted the soft-drink can to his lips and took a deep drink. "Andy and I were never very close to our parents. I know Molly's withdrawal the past week has her more worried than anything else. She doesn't want her daughter to grow up as lonely and as uncommunicative as we were with our parents."

Jessica held her breath. *Please, go on.*

Karl didn't seem to be able to stop. "We had everything kids could ever want. My father was a self-made man who worked at changing his millions into billions. We never lacked for anything." Karl's voice sloped off, dwindled to a whisper. "Except love."

The pain came through clearly. Jessica's heart spasmed at the void in Karl's childhood.

"Was he too busy?" Jessica asked gently.

"It wasn't only that. He didn't know how to show love. He'd never been on the receiving end of any as a child, and he thought expressions of love were superfluous. He worked hard, provided for us, and that was it. Andy and I grew up thinking it was the right way to live. My mother suffered the most. I remember when I was younger how hard she tried to make everything seem normal, cover for my father, but as I grew up, she became more and more withdrawn herself. I was in high school before I realized how much she'd suffered because of his coldness. The amazing thing is they're still together, though they don't seem to have the slightest interest in each other.''

Jessica didn't say a word. To interject anything now might stop the flow of Karl's confidences.

''I thought everyone's families were like that, till I visited a friend of mine when I was ten. That weekend showed me a whole new way of life. I saw the way a family *could* be. The Garrisons communicated with hugs and kisses as much as they did with words. It wasn't only the physical demonstrations of love that made such an impression—it was the way they cared about whatever was happening to one of them. There was laughter in that home, happiness you could reach out and touch. It was a real revelation. I didn't want to go home after that visit. I wanted to be the Garrisons' son so badly, it hurt. I never went back there. Ben Garrison couldn't understand why I wouldn't accept his invitations for the weekend after that one time.''

Karl picked up a shell and examined it while he continued. ''I realized something then. Love isn't rationed or something that's allotted from above. It's free. People avail of it as they wish. Their use of it is shaped by their own experiences, their mental makeup. My father didn't think it was important at all. I watched my mother give up the struggle to keep things normal, withdraw from all of us, grow old before her time. She didn't deserve treatment like that. No woman does. I didn't realize how badly Andy felt the lack of harmony between our parents till she left home. She was always getting into trouble at home and at school. I was too young to know it was her way of asking for attention. She left home at eighteen, without telling anyone where she was going.''

Karl picked up another shell, searched the smooth surface for answers to the puzzles of human behavior. ''She took off for New York, got in with a bad crowd. Luckily she met Jim before she came to any real harm. Marrying him was the turning point in her life. Jim and Molly mean everything in the world to her. I don't want her happiness endangered.''

He turned to look at the little girl with the huge dog, prancing in the shallows, running ahead of the waves. The bleakness in his eyes revealed his own unhappiness yet untended.

''When you marry and have your children,'' Jessica began softly, his pain a throb in her throat, ''you'll find by loving your family that you heal some of your own hurts.''

Where had that come from? Surprise prompted Jessica to close her mouth. Maybe she ought to apply for Ann Landers's job. Karl looked out at the water. Jessica stole a glance at his face. Her last remark hadn't even made a dent in the hard wall of his memories.

''Karl . . .'' She had to apologize for preaching.

''Jessica,'' he began, unaware he'd interrupted her. ''I don't know if I will ever marry. Deep down inside is this fear there's too much of my father in me. I've never been able to feel deeply enough for a woman to warrant marriage. I've had so many women friends. I've cared about them. I've never loved them.''

He stated it coolly, as if he'd already planned his life around the thought. Stunned, Jessica lifted a handful of sand and watched it dribble through her fingers. Convincing Karl he was excellent family material wouldn't be easy. But someone had to do it.

Not *someone*. Her. This was a challenge she couldn't turn her back on.

Karl was a wonderful human being. The fact that no one had ever awakened that part of him to do with real caring didn't mean the part was missing.

She'd have to be careful, though. Karl hadn't been aware he was telling her anything about himself. Only concern over his sister and Molly had prompted the confidence. If she went about this clumsily, Karl might withdraw completely. And that couldn't be.

"Uncle Karl, Jessica, aren't you coming in?" Molly rushed up impatiently. "The water's really warm."

"Be right there." As his niece ran off again, Karl stood up, slipped out of his shorts and took his shirt off. His red swimming trunks accentuated his lithe physique perfectly.

He held a hand out to Jessica. She put her hand in his, wondering what he was going to think of her misty purple bathing suit. The tug on her hand brought her up to within an inch of his bare chest. Jessica stepped back quickly. There was a great deal of Karl Wagner, and there wasn't much of her. Covered or uncovered. Someone hadn't been fair distributing physical attributes.

They walked to the water's edge hand in hand. Jessica was conscious of the thump of her heart over the swish of the waves, the screams of some voluptuous bikini-clad volleyball players close by, the tangy smell of the ocean. Jessica jumped as the first wave garlanded her feet with an icy offering.

"Ooh!"

Karl's hand tightened around hers. The grin he gave her made her heart exchange wild thumping for mad cartwheels. This was the Karl she wanted to see. Carefree, happy, lighthearted.

"You'll get used to it," he promised as he tugged her farther in.

It wasn't till a wave caught her chest-high that Jessica realized something. Karl was paying no more attention to the scantily clad volleyball players than Arthur was. The young women had the kind of bodies that men came to the beach to ogle, but his whole attention was on her and Molly as if no one else was around. Thinking of the dates who had brought her to the beach and then spent the entire time scanning the area like hungry wolves, Jessica wanted to throw her arms around Karl and kiss him for being so special.

He hadn't commented on her suit, but Molly had.

"I like you in that color, Jessica," she'd yelled when they had joined her.

"Th-thanks." Jessica's stammer had betrayed her shyness. Awareness that Karl's intent gaze was fixed on her made her tingle from head to toe.

"Uncle Karl, don't you like Jessica's bathing suit?" Molly asked mock-innocently. "Remember what you said last year when we came to California on vacation and you brought us to the beach? That you didn't know if beachwear these days was meant to cover anything or merely to draw attention to how much was uncovered. You said there was something ugly in overexposure. Jessica's bathing suit isn't like that."

Jessica stood stock-still and stared at Karl. His skin turned red as he glared at his niece.

"Were those remarks addressed to you, young lady?" he asked.

Not a whit abashed, Molly looked straight at him. "No. You and Daddy were talking, and I heard."

"As you manage to hear everything else you're not supposed to," he said.

Suddenly Jessica felt very, very lighthearted. It was fun to be at the beach on such a wonderful day. She no longer felt awkward about her demure one-piece bathing suit. In fact she felt very good in it. Maybe she had a fairy godmother, after all.

"Look out, you two!" Karl's shout made her look up in time to see the wall of water coming toward them. With a purely reflex action she turned into his chest. The wave drenched all three of them from head to toe. Karl seemed in no hurry to let her go. Jessica wondered if she'd imagined the slight tightening of his grip.

Karl appeared to have got over being annoyed with Molly. "Let's see how your swimming's coming along, Molly," he told her, letting go of a wriggling Jessica slowly.

They lingered in the water till Molly complained of hunger. The picnic lunch was more than enough for all three of them. Arthur got a few tidbits, as well. They repacked every bit of trash, and then Molly ran off to build a sand castle with Arthur.

Karl suppressed a yawn and apologized. "I'm sorry. I was up at five to take Arthur for his morning run, and the ocean air always makes me sleepy."

"Why don't you take a nap?" Jessica suggested comfortably. "I'll watch Molly."

"Are you sure?" Karl hesitated, his eyes growing heavier with every passing second.

"Positive."

He stretched out on his stomach and buried his face in his hands.

Jessica let the magazine she'd been reading fall and studied Karl's prone figure thoughtfully. The conversation they had had earlier returned to haunt her. Her eyes lingered on every visible sinew of his brown body as she thought of a way to help him. It was so unfair. There was really no reason the specter of his past should throw its dark shadow over the present and the future. She thought of him as a young boy, lonely and sad, and her heart spasmed with pain.

Molly's laugh carried back to Jessica. The group she'd teamed up with had abandoned the sand castle for burying a patient Arthur in sand.

It didn't make sense that someone as loving and as patient as Karl should doubt his abilities to be a good parent. But these days psychologists spoke of deep traits buried in people that only emerged with their immediate families. Jessica thought of the television series she'd watched about famous people and abuse. There was the judge who abused his wife. The teacher who beat her own children. The doctor who was an alcoholic. None of their families had talked about their problems. Loyalty, shame and a misplaced sense of duty were powerful silencers.

A gull edged up to the picnic basket, one inquisitive eye fixed on Jessica.

Did Karl really believe he was capable of emotional abuse? That marriage would open up some dark side of him? Jessica blinked. It just wasn't possible. Not Karl. He was too sensitive to ever cause others pain. He'd proved it over and over again since they'd first met. Fierce determination surged in her to convince him of the fact.

"Have you found another dog to champion?"

Jessica jumped. Karl's head was turned sideways on his arms, and he was watching her. She blushed. How long had he been awake?

"Excuse me?"

"I asked you if you'd found another dog to champion."

"No. Why do you ask?"

"You had that same *do-or-die* expression on your face as you did the day I saw you with Arthur."

Jessica slipped into her shirt and concentrated on fastening the buttons. "It's nothing," she muttered.

Karl didn't pursue the topic. Sitting up with one lithe movement, he looked at his watch as Molly ran up to them and took a soft-drink can out of the cooler. Jessica longed to lean toward him and brush the fine golden sand from his skin.

"Molly, five minutes more, and we have to be going," Karl said.

"Aw, Uncle Karl." She took a long sip of her drink.

"You don't want Arthur to catch a cold again, do you?"

"I'll be ready in five minutes," Molly said immediately. "I just have to say goodbye to my friends."

Jessica stood up and walked over to the children with Molly. She needed a few minutes away from Karl to marshal her scattered senses into some kind of order before she got into the close confines of the car with him.

A worn-out Arthur and Molly fell asleep on the way home. Sand-cased limbs, sun-soaked bodies and the look on their faces testified to a day filled with fun.

Jessica turned to Karl. It was time for more important things. If she waited too long, she might not find the right moment. Checking over her shoulder to see if Molly really was asleep, Jessica took a deep breath.

"Summer wants to marry you when she grows up," she began.

"Who?" Karl flashed her a look of amazement.

"Summer," repeated Jessica politely. "A little girl... about so high. Her mother mentioned seventeen fillings?"

"Summer Kennedy." Realization dawned, accompanied by a huge smile. "She's a real heartbreaker."

Jessica wasn't about to be deterred by a discussion about Summer. "Her mother couldn't say enough good things about you."

Karl shrugged. "Mrs. Kennedy's just grateful Summer's treatment went so well. Cavities like her little girl had can cause future complications."

Jessica wasn't prepared to discuss cavities or grateful mothers just yet, either.

"Mrs. Lucas, your office manager, thinks the world of you, too."

He was beginning to tune into the fact that her conversation had a purpose.

"So does Molly," continued Jessica. "So does Arthur."

So do I. The words were barely caught back in time.

"Yes." His tone told her to hurry up and get to the point.

She had to say it now while she still could. Already Karl's tone was proving a serious deterrent.

"You can fool a grown-up, but you can never ever fool a child or a dog," stated Jessica flatly. "You can buy a grown-up's affection, sometimes even a child's, never an animal's."

"All right, Jessica." His sigh wasn't discouraging. The smile in his voice came through clearly. "Let it out. What's bothering you?"

"What I'm trying to say is, I don't understand how, when you have the capacity for inspiring so much love, you can doubt your own ability to give it." She spoiled it all by ending on a quaver.

Those unreliable, idiotic, overactive tear ducts.

His brows snapped together. Jessica's heart skipped a beat. She'd again charged in where angels refused to tread.

"Traits like I mentioned don't always show, Jessica," Karl said without anger. "When we had our friends over as children, my father could have put a television-show parent in the shade. He would hand out candy, tell a few jokes, take us down to the ice-cream parlor. Appearances were important to him. But when we were on our own, it was so different. Never a word of encouragement, of love, and always that terrible coldness toward my mother. I asked her about it once. She said he'd had a terribly unhappy childhood. I couldn't understand why he was punishing her and, indirectly, us for it. I understand better now, but I still don't accept why."

He stopped at a traffic light, but didn't turn his head to look at her. "Only someone who's been there can guess at the tremendous strain unhappy parents put on their children. What if I *am* like my father? Molly, Arthur, little Summer—they're not really mine. I see Mrs. Lucas only for a few hours each day. It's easy to be kind to other people's kids, to men and women you see for a while. The real test is to be kind to those closest to you."

"You *are* kind," Jessica protested as they stopped at another traffic light.

Karl didn't seem to hear. "Doesn't everyone put on a different cloak when they go to work? Assume a different personality from their normal one? Well, I've never taken that cloak off with anyone...I'm terrified to. I can't risk waiting till I marry to discover I'm a clone of my father. I can't risk history repeating itself."

The lights changed, and Karl accelerated. Jessica kept quiet. She could see he was really upset. It didn't show in his face or his voice, but the hands that clutched the steering wheel had white knuckles. Arguing the point any more right now might turn off the friendliness completely. She couldn't risk that. She had to make sure the door stayed open so she could work on this chip on his shoulder again.

Chip? It was a rock really. It made the one in Gibraltar seem like a pebble.

It wasn't till late that night that Jessica remembered she hadn't thanked Karl for the flowers he'd sent her on Valentine's Day. Maybe she ought to simply send him a thank-you card.

She was floundering in something. Substance that looked like yellow jelly wouldn't let her get free. Every time Jessica tried to extricate herself, it sucked her in deeper. She was trapped. Someone was coming toward her. She could sense the menace. He held a bell in one hand and he kept ringing it. Louder and louder.

It wasn't a bell. It was the telephone on her nightstand.

"Hello?" Drat the whole pizza she'd devoured. It always gave her nightmares. She could never resist it, though.

"Jessica, Andy's just been taken to the hospital." Karl's clipped tones made her jump out of bed. "Molly's hysterical. Jim called me a minute ago from the hospital. Their neighbors are with Molly, but Jim isn't sure if they can handle her. Will you come with me?"

Two a.m. Poor Andy and Jim. *Please don't let them lose the baby.* Poor Molly. The intelligent ones always saw more, suffered more.

"I'm on my way." She'd already slid into a pair of jeans. Finding a shirt, washing her face and brushing her teeth would take three minutes. In Jessica's large family, getting ready in record time had become an acquired skill.

"Thanks, Jessica."

It was Thursday. Four days since she'd gone to the beach with him and Molly. Four long, empty days.

Jessica's hands tightened on the wheel. This wasn't the time to be thinking of the way she felt.

The garage door went up silently, and Karl pulled the Audi out as she parked her car in front of his house. Jessica locked her car and got into Karl's. The leather felt cool at her back.

"Jessica, thanks for coming so quickly." He was already reversing, his attention on the road behind him.

"Hello, Karl."

He didn't say anything more, just picked up her hand and squeezed it. Jessica felt a lump the size of the Rose Bowl well up in her throat. Trite words of consolation would almost be an insult. They wouldn't express her understanding of the deep fear in Karl's heart. She stayed silent.

Nothing's going to happen to Andy or the baby, Jessica told herself fiercely. She pictured a woman who was an older version of Molly, holding a baby, smiling happily, her family bunched around her. That's how it had to be.

Please, let it be like that.

Vibrations of fear and helplessness snaked out from Karl to her. He was afraid he'd lose his sister. He was afraid Andy would lose the baby. He was afraid, period.

"I can stay with Molly, and you could go to the hospital and be with Jim." Being there would make the waiting easier for Karl.

For the first time that night she had his total attention. "Are you sure?"

"Yes." It might alleviate some of his tension. Besides, she was sure Andy's husband could do with some company right now.

Karl pulled up in front of the apartment building. "I'll introduce you to the Macauleys first and see how Molly is. Jim said Andy's anxious about her."

Molly flung herself on her uncle as soon as he unlocked and opened the door. She raised a blotchy red face to ask, "Is my mommy all right?"

Karl made no effort to hide the tears in his own eyes. "I hope so, sweetheart." The hand that caressed his niece's blond head trembled slightly. "I certainly hope so." Picking up Molly, he held her close, as much for his own sake as for hers.

And this was the man who said he never took his outer cloak off with anyone? He might not be aware of it, but it was off now. Jessica looked away, blinking rapidly. The naked stamp of pain and fear on Karl's face was almost her undoing. This was no time for tears. She had to be strong for them.

"Tina and Brian, this is Jessica Hansen, a friend of mine. Jessica, meet Tina and Brian Macauley. They're Andy and Jim's neighbors and good friends." He set Molly down but held her hand. "Jessica will stay with Molly now. Thanks for being here."

The young couple nodded and stood up, their faces lined with worry. "We're glad we could help. Our number's by the telephone. Let us know as soon as there's news. If there's anything else we can do..."

"Thanks. We'll be sure and let you know." Karl saw them to the door, then closed it behind them.

He turned to see Jessica on the couch. Molly sat on her lap, sobbing into her shoulder. Jessica didn't say a word, just sat there rubbing Molly's back, her own mouth aquiver with emotion. Though she wasn't much bigger than Molly physically, she was all woman as she consoled the frightened child. Karl struggled with the need to haul them both to his chest, hold them close to his heart.

He cleared his throat. "Molly, honey, would you like me to go to the hospital and find out how your mommy's doing?"

The tears stopped. Molly lifted her head off Jessica's shoulder. "Can I come, too?"

"No, honey." He reached a hand up and brushed the hair off her hot forehead and let his hand rest on Jessica's shoulder. His thumb massaged her collarbone. She wasn't sure if the contact was for her comfort or for his. "They won't let kids in at this hour to visit.

Indecision hovered on Molly's face. Then she turned to the couch. "Will you stay with me, Jessica?"

"For as long as it takes, Molly."

Molly nodded and said, "Promise you'll call as soon as you get there?"

"Promise." He was already halfway to the door.

Jessica and Molly looked at each other as it locked behind him.

"Want to talk about it?" Jessica asked gently.

The tears ran down Molly's face unchecked. "I heard noises and woke up. Mommy's back was hurting very bad, she told me. Daddy said the doctor wanted to examine Mommy, so they had to go to the hospital. Then the ambulance came, and they told me to stay out of the way like a good girl."

It didn't take a genius to guess how the sight of the paramedics, the wail of the siren, would have frightened Molly.

"They probably called an ambulance because it gets you to the hospital in the shortest possible time," Jessica said quietly. "There were nine of us at home when my father had his heart attack. It was a small one, but we still called an ambulance because we wanted him to have the best of care on the way to the hospital and get there in the quickest time possible. On the way to the hospital he had another big heart attack. The paramedics saved his life because they had all the equipment and the know-how."

Molly wiped a tear away with the back of her hand. "Daddy called just before you and Uncle Karl got here. He said the doctors were with Mommy and he was waiting outside."

"Karl's going to call us very soon," Jessica reminded as Molly's mouth wobbled again. "Maybe he'll even be able to see your mommy by the time he gets there."

Molly looked at the kitchen clock and sniffed. "How long will it take?"

"Let's see. It takes twenty minutes to get to St. Mary's from here." The hospital was only five minutes away, but the extra time would prevent Molly from worrying. "Then another twenty minutes to find out what's happening. That's forty minutes altogether. Sometimes, too, the phones are tied up by other people calling their families, so let's allow another ten minutes for that. I'm sure he'll call by three-fifteen."

Molly looked at the clock again, then sat down on the couch. Jessica's heart contracted at the woebegone expression on Molly's face. She wondered what she could do to help ease the pain.

"Would it be okay if I got myself a glass of milk?" Jessica asked gently.

Molly nodded. "Sure."

Jessica opened the refrigerator and spotted what she was looking for right away. Molly's parents had the same squeeze plastic container of drinking chocolate in their refrigerator as Karl had in his. "Want to join me for some hot chocolate?"

Molly looked at her thoughtfully over the back of the couch. The mention of hot chocolate worked. She got off the couch and came to the kitchen. "Okay."

"You'll have to show me how to use your microwave. The controls are different."

Molly helped get the chocolate ready and even found some marshmallows. They sat at the table sipping the beverage, and Jessica hoped the warm milk would help calm Molly. Instead, Jessica saw worry slither into the eight-year-old's eyes again, the tremor of her bottom lip.

"Did I tell you about my second dog, Trucker?"

Molly nodded. She'd enjoyed the stories of Trucker and the mailman's feud. "Do you remember some more things he did?"

Jessica nodded. "Once, my sister Sara got stuck in an old apple tree at the back of our yard and no one even guessed she was missing. But Trucker knew. He caught hold of my Mom's skirt in his teeth and almost dragged her to the apple tree.''

"How old was your sister?"

"Sara was about fourteen. She'd just decided to climb that old tree and then couldn't get down."

The phone rang. Molly darted to it and picked it up. "Uncle Karl, how's my mommy?"

Stomach knotted, Jessica watched the pixielike face as the little girl listened intently. "She is? She said that?" Each comment was lighter than the last. It had to be good news. Jessica felt the knot in her stomach ease. "Where's my daddy? Hi, Dad. Is Mommy really all right? Yes, Daddy. Yes. I love you, too, Daddy. I *am* being brave, Daddy. Will you give Mommy a kiss from me, right in the middle of her forehead? Tell her I love her? Bye, Daddy." Molly turned and held the phone out to Jessica. Her smile scotched all doubts that it wasn't good news. "Uncle Karl wants to talk to you. Mommy's doing fine."

"Jessica." The honey-warm tones of Karl's voice dissolved the distance between them. "Andy is doing fine. The doctor's decided to remove the baby by C-section, though."

"I see."

"The baby will be four weeks premature, but the obstetrician says there's a ninety-nine percent chance everything is going to be fine." Already he sounded more like himself.

"That's great." Tears edged into her eyes.

"How are you and Molly doing?" There was enough warmth in his tone to melt the Poles. And the man feared he would be too cold in a personal relationship? *Humbug.* "I can come back and get her and take her to my place, so you can go home and get some sleep."

"You stay right where you are, Karl Wagner," Jessica ordered huskily. "I'm where I want to be. Call us as soon as you hear something. Molly and I are doing fine."

"Thanks, Jessica. Goodbye for now," he said, then broke the connection.

"I can't sleep till Mommy's had the baby," Molly announced semifirmly, watching Jessica's face for a reaction.

"Of course you can't," Jessica agreed. She figured Jim Spencer had told his daughter to go to bed. This wasn't a night for enforcing parental rules, though. The VCR gave her an idea. "Why don't we sit down and watch *The Sound of Music*?"

Molly had mentioned receiving the video cassette of the movie as a present for Valentine's Day. It might make the waiting less of an ordeal.

"I'll put the tape in." Molly loaded the tape and came over to the couch, remote control in hand.

Jessica spread the afghan over both of them. Molly cuddled up to her side, suppressing a yawn. The first song on the mountains was barely over when a soft snore attracted Jessica's attention. Molly was fast asleep.

She waited a while before laying Molly down, placing a cushion under her head. Tucking the afghan carefully around the girl, she beamed her request upward.

Please let her wake up to good news and happiness.

Chapter Seven

It was close to the end of the movie when Jessica heard the key turn in the lock. Unwilling to disturb Molly, she stayed where she was.

Karl came in, stopped short at the sight of them and looked his fill. The glow on his face told its own story.

"Andy's fine." Kneeling in front of the couch, he took Jessica's hands in his. "A baby boy. Five pounds. They are both doing well."

The muscles in his cheeks quivered. Jessica knew he was having a hard time trying not to give in to his emotions. She didn't say a word. She simply drew Karl's head to her chest, wrapped both arms around him, rested her cheek against the top of his head and let the tears she'd held back all evening flow. Karl's arms went around her, and he said, "Jessica, I was so scared...."

"I know." She wound her fingers through his hair, caressed his scalp, not quite aware of what she was doing.

Relief was weightless. It took the place of their unvoiced fears, intoxicated them with its heady potency.

"Is Mommy okay?" As quickly as she'd fallen asleep, Molly was awake.

Karl lifted his head, leaned back on his haunches and held his arms out to his niece. "She's fine. You can see her this afternoon."

"What about the baby?" Instead of going into her uncle's arms, Molly leaned back against the cushions.

"A baby boy. He's fine, too."

"I'm glad." Molly stood, half-asleep, and gathered the afghan around her. "Now maybe we can all get some sleep. I know I'm going to look awful tomorrow."

They watched her trail into her bedroom and waited for the door to shut before they burst out laughing.

"That's it?" demanded Karl incredulously. "I thought we were going to have more tears."

"Happiness takes many forms," Jessica said between chuckles. "Right now Molly's still half-asleep."

"You didn't get a wink of sleep yourself, did you?" His attention strayed to the television screen. *The Sound of Music.* He looked at Jessica and traced a tear mark with his finger. "Do you always believe in happily-ever-after, Jessica?"

He wasn't talking about movies. The wistfulness in his tone told Jessica he was talking about life. About believing. "Always."

The silence pooled around them, then Karl got to his feet. "I mustn't keep you up any longer. Do you have to go to work today?"

Jessica shook her head and said, "I'm going to take the day off and catch up on my sleep."

Karl glanced at her mouth, then away. She wished he wouldn't keep doing that.

"I'm going to take Molly to my place and crash for a few hours. Then I have to go into the clinic for a couple of hours at least. Jim is going to stay at the hospital. Nothing will drag him away from there. Andy has a private room, and they've put in an extra bed for him."

"Why don't we all stay right here?" Jessica suggested. "That way you won't have to wake up Molly again or worry about finding someone to watch her. You can leave whenever you want to in the morning, and I'll stay with Molly till either you or Jim get back."

"We've already imposed on you enough."

"I was glad to help," Jessica said briskly. "Why don't you wash up while I find something to eat? You'll sleep better on a full stomach."

She held her breath. Was she being too bossy all of a sudden? She just wanted to take care of him while he was so tired.

Karl hesitated, then smiled. "Yes, ma'am."

Jessica poached a couple of eggs, put frozen hash brown potatoes into the microwave with a pat of butter and made some toast. By the time Karl came out of the bathroom, everything was ready.

"Aren't you having any?" He sat down and frowned at the solitary place setting.

"I will later." Jessica stood by the table, hoping Karl would like the way she'd fixed the eggs.

"Don't wait for me to eat," Karl said. "The linen closet's by the bathroom, if you don't mind changing your own sheets. Use Andy and Jim's room. I've put one of my shirts on the bed in there for you to wear."

"Of course I don't mind changing the sheets. I'll see you later, then."

He looked at the plate and then up at her. When he reached for her hands, she blinked. Now what? Through a haze she watched him lift her hands to his mouth and press his lips against each set of fingers in turn.

"Thank you for everything."

She stood there like a frozen rabbit, ignoring the overdose of adrenaline coursing through her body. She felt beautiful. Ten feet tall, graceful, *breathtaking*.

"Go to bed, Jessica," Karl said softly. "You're half-asleep."

She backed away from the table without taking her eyes from him, then turned abruptly and fled.

The first closed door she knew was Molly's; the second was the bathroom. The third had to be the master bedroom. She went in, shut the door, leaned against it and closed her eyes.

She wanted to hold this feeling close to her heart for today. Tomorrow she would try to decipher all the scrambled messages in her brain.

Jessica's eyes closed the minute she lay down. Sleep was a fog that claimed her immediately. It had to be her imagination that someone was tucking her in, bending to press a kiss to her cheek and saying softly, "Sweet dreams, sweetheart."

There *was* someone in her room. Jessica stiffened. Opening one eye slowly, she looked at the beige walls, the Monet posters in oak frames. The events of the past several hours came flooding back. Molly had a new baby brother. Karl had kissed her hands, made her feel like a princess.

Molly smiled guilelessly up at her from her place on the foot of the bed. "I was waiting for you to wake up," she said virtuously. "Do you know Mommy's had the baby? His name's Richard Karl. Uncle Karl said he told me last night, but I don't remember."

Jessica smiled, remembering Molly's comments the night before. "Yes, he did."

"We're going to see Mommy this afternoon. I think I should wear a dress. Nana always says dresses are for important occasions. What do you think, Jessica?"

"I think a dress would be very nice."

"Please will you take me to a florist so I can pick out some flowers to take Mommy?"

"Of course. Where's Uncle Karl?"

"He left when I woke up this morning. There's a note for you." Molly jerked her head toward the nightstand.

Karl had written in a neat flowing hand:

Jessica
I've left the Audi for you. If you don't mind, would you please take Molly back to my house whenever you're ready? I'll meet you there by two at the latest.

He must have taken a cab to work. Nervousness assailed her at the thought of driving Karl's expensive car. Being trusted with a man's car, according to her brother David, was a high honor. Jessica wasn't sure she wanted the honor. A woman with a fairy godmother who didn't show up regularly had to be extra careful.

"What time is it, do you know?" she asked Molly.

"It's twelve. I talked to Mommy in the hospital, and Daddy called me half an hour ago. I finished watching *The Sound of Music* this morning. Then I lay down by you because I was sleepy. Shall I fix you some of my special muffins while you get dressed?"

This was the old Molly. Confident, happy, *in charge*.

"Please."

Smiling, Jessica went into the bathroom and pulled on her jeans. She'd removed them last night and had slept in her long green shirt. If she'd put on Karl's shirt, she would never have been able to sleep. Simply picking it up and holding it to her cheek had been excitement enough.

Jessica grimaced at her reflection. She needed a shower and a change of clothes, but that would have to wait till she got to her apartment. Squeezing some toothpaste onto her finger, Jessica set about freshening up before they left.

They stopped off at the apartment first. Molly was thrilled with Jessica's place. She went around the living room looking at everything.

"Why don't you call your dad and let him know where we are while I hit the shower?" Jessica suggested. "There are some oatmeal cookies in the teddy bear cookie jar on the counter, milk in the refrigerator. Help yourself to whatever you want."

"Okay." Molly studied the collage of family pictures on the wall with great interest.

After her shower Jessica pulled on a lavender jumpsuit with a purple sash and fastened purple circles in her ears. Standing back, she surveyed the effect. Her best wasn't anything spectacular. At least her glasses minimized the effect of the dark circles.

"Jessica, can I come in now?" Molly called through the closed door.

"Sure."

Molly wandered in and looked around the bedroom with open curiosity. "I called Daddy," she threw over her shoulder. "He said Uncle Karl's going to take us to the hospital around three o'clock. We can't stay too long, though, because Mommy needs to rest. Daddy said he called Nana in England, and she and Gramps are leaving as soon as they can get tickets. Nana's going to take care of Mommy and the baby till Mommy gets really strong again."

"Your Nana sounds very special." Jessica wondered why there was no mention of the other set of grandparents.

"She is—" Molly nodded "—and she smells so good." A small silence followed. "When I was born, she came and stayed in New York for three months to help Mommy. We go to England every other year, and they come here the other times. Nana knows lots of nice stories and she doesn't get cross if you get dirty."

"Sounds like my kind of grandmother."

Molly nodded. "Gramps is fun, too. He takes me fishing and tells me stories about the Second World War. He was in the British Army before he retired and opened a bookstore in Sussex."

Molly had her nose pressed to the window and was watching the courtyard below. "Your mailman's here," she announced, and then went on casually. "You know I love Grandpa and Grandma Wagner, too. They always send me money at Christmas and dolls from all over the world, but I think I love Nana and Gramps more." Looking straight at Jessica, she elaborated. "You can touch them."

Out of the mouths of eight-year-olds, thought Jessica, picking up the keys to Karl's Audi.

Karl was already at the house. "Hi!" he greeted them, smiling. "How's the big sister?" He swung Molly up in the air. When her feet touched ground, she raced off to find Arthur. "How are you, Jessica?"

"I'm fine." She shifted from one foot to the other. The bright light of day robbed her of the illusions of the night before. Gratitude under duress didn't translate into love the next morning. "Well, I think I'll get back now."

She hoped her old car wouldn't disgrace her by not starting. Driving Karl's car had been a wonderful experience.

Karl looked surprised. "Aren't you coming with us to the hospital to see the baby?"

"Of course not!" said Jessica emphatically. "This is a family occasion."

"Andy wants to meet you." Karl took one of her curled fists in his and embarked on his guerrilla warfare approach. As his thumb flirted with her palm, her heart broke into a wild gallop. "Unless you're tired and want to rest?"

Jessica didn't know what to say. Her brain was being overloaded with confusing messages again. She doubted that excitement would allow her to sleep for the next twenty-four hours.

"I've made a special lunch," coaxed Karl. "At least eat with us before you make a decision."

What was it about him this afternoon? Jessica wondered. She knew he was happy about his sister's safe delivery and having a nephew, but the glow on his face was more than all that combined. It seemed a reflection of some deep inner happiness.

Arthur and Molly raced around the side of the house and skidded to a halt right in front of them.

"I forgot my flowers," said Molly. "They're still in the car."

"I'll get them out for you," Jessica said. She needed time to organize her thoughts. Picking up the pot of violets in the pretty ceramic container, as well as Molly's overnight bag, Jessica turned.

"Let me take that from you." Karl slipped his fingers between the strap and her shoulder and removed Molly's bag.

Jessica trembled as Karl's gaze focused on her mouth.

"Uncle Karl, look at my flowers. Do you like them? Jessica said this way Mommy would have something that lasts longer."

"Jessica has very good taste," Karl said approvingly, his gaze still on Jessica.

"Jessica, are you going to come with us to the hospital to meet Mommy and the baby?"

Jessica looked at Molly's expectant face. "You know this is a special time for family to be together," she said gently. "Maybe I can visit on the weekend or after the baby comes home."

Molly didn't argue with that. She just flashed her uncle a glance and turned away into the house. "I'm going to talk to Arthur about the baby," she announced. "If I let him in on everything from the start, he's not going to be jealous of the baby."

Karl's brows were raised high as his gaze quizzed Jessica's face. She clung to the open rear door of the Audi for dear life, refusing to laugh. Humor wasn't going to divert her this time.

"I really have to be going now." As their gazes meshed, Jessica recalled the good-night kiss. It hadn't been imagination. It had been Karl. As the memory of him carefully tucking her in flooded her mind, Jessica's heart accelerated to its now familiar calypso rhythm.

He stepped forward and bent his head. "Sweet Jessica," he murmured, a tormenting fraction away from her lips.

"Excuse me, please!" Molly's voice was an unwanted wedge between them.

They both turned their heads to look at her. Jessica wondered if imagination supplied Karl's sigh. Molly held a cordless telephone out to her. "Daddy's on the telephone and he wants to talk to you, Jessica."

"To me?"

She looked at Karl. A shrug was his only response as she took the phone from Molly.

"Hello?"

"Jessica!" Warmth spiced with a British accent poured over the phone. "Jim Spencer, here. How are you?"

"Fi-fine, thank you, Mr. Spencer."

"Please call me Jim," Molly's father requested. "I won't keep you long. My wife and I just want to thank you for being Molly's friend and to say how much we look forward to meeting you this afternoon."

Jessica looked at Molly. Her angelic expression gave nothing of her schemes away. Karl's niece had a great future in the diplomatic service.

There was nothing she could say except a weak, "Me, too."

"Great! Is Karl there?"

Jessica handed Karl the telephone and stood in the sunshine, staring at the begonia in the flower beds.

"Let's go in and have some lunch, then we can leave for the hospital," he said after a few minutes.

Jessica looked down at her clothes. "I'm not dressed right," she muttered to herself.

Karl caught the words and stopped to look at her in amazement. "Of course you are!" he said. "You're perfect!"

There were two kinds of perfect. Perfect as in it-doesn't-really-matter perfect, or the perfect-for-me perfect. Jessica wondered which was Karl's perfect.

Jessica found Molly talking to Arthur in the family room. "Daddy says we're going to move into the house before Mommy gets out of the hospital. You're coming, too. We'll be together every day." Arthur put out a huge tongue and licked Molly's face. "Have you seen a baby before, Arthur? Daddy says you have to be very careful around the baby, or you might have to be kept in your dog run all the time."

"Woof." The deep rumble had Molly giggling. Encouraged, the Great Dane put one huge forepaw on either side of the couch and licked her face again. Molly's thin arms circled the dog's neck, and she hugged him tight.

Jessica watched Karl remove some French bread from the oven and slice it. He'd mentioned the house Molly's parents had bought in the city of Walnut, ten minutes away. Arthur would be gone soon. Jessica wondered what would happen then. Would she ever see Karl again? Her throat constricted.

The future didn't beckon. It threatened like rain-packed clouds.

"Let's eat. Molly, go wash up." Karl set the shrimp salad on the table, next to the bread basket. "Will you have some coffee?"

"No, thanks."

A future without Karl seemed bleak and lonely. Would he simply return to his old way of life, settle back into ways he had no intention of changing after Arthur was gone?

It's a free country, remember? There's nothing you can do really if the man chooses to remain single.

Suddenly cold, Jessica shivered.

"May I be excused, please?"

Jessica looked up in surprise. Molly had cleaned her plate in record time. Her own bore a pile of crumbled bread and a moved-around shrimp salad. Karl was treating her to one of his gimlet glances.

"Don't you like it?"

"It's delicious." Hurriedly she picked up a forkful and carried it to her mouth to prove her point.

"Are you upset about something?" he asked.

"No."

"What is it, then?" He reached for her hand.

"It's nothing." It was hard to look into Rocky Mountain eyes and lie.

Karl's eyes began to glitter. "You don't like having your mind being made up for you, remember? Are you resenting that, maybe?" His thumb caressed the inside of her wrist, making her pulse riot.

Jessica pushed her chair back and rose to her feet. Her mind scrambled for reasons and came up blank. "I was just wondering what to get your sister and the baby." A decision surfaced. "In fact I think I'll go pick up something now and meet you at the hospital."

Karl frowned. "We could stop off on the way to the hospital if you feel you *have* to get something."

"I'd rather just meet you there."

Karl searched her face and then nodded. "Fine. It's quarter to two now. If we meet at three in the east parking lot of St. Mary's, will that give you enough time?"

"Yes." Jessica picked up her plate to put it in the sink, but Karl stopped her with a touch on her wrist. "Leave it. I'm just going to put everything in the dishwasher."

"I'll see you later, then." Would she ever get over this odd reluctance to leave him?

"Drive carefully."

Jessica tried to concentrate on gifts as she drove off. She had no idea what to get Molly's mother. Frantically she tried to remember what Molly had mentioned her mother liked. Nothing came to mind. There were so many things for babies in the market these days. Hopefully a shop assistant would be able to help her choose something.

Jessica's mind returned to dwell on the feel of Karl's hands. They could have her from sane to crazy in thirty seconds. As for his mouth . . . it ought to be cited a fire hazard.

The signs were all there. She'd seen them so many times before. They'd always made her want to run. Except that this time she was running *toward*—not away. She didn't feel threatened by Karl.

Jessica took a deep breath. So, she wanted more with Karl Wagner. The question was, was he willing to give anything more?

Seeing the sign for the east parking lot of the hospital, Jessica shelved her thoughts temporarily and concentrated on finding a place to park.

Karl and Molly were waiting for her in the lot.

"Got what you wanted?" He opened the car door for her.

The port-a-crib she'd picked out was the latest one on the market, according to the salesperson in the baby store. It folded into a compact rectangle, easy to carry around.

"Yes, thank you." Jessica got out of the car and looked at Molly, who was anxiously waiting to be noticed. "Molly, you look beautiful. I love your dress."

Her hair was brushed out and a ribbon tied in it. The pink-and-white dress made Jessica long for a girl of her own to dress and to share secrets with.

"Jessica, will you check my bow, please?" She turned her head so that Jessica could see the pink ribbon in her hair. "Uncle Karl isn't sure he got it right."

Karl smiled at Jessica. "Don't have any experience in that department. Sorry."

A pulse leaped into a break dance in Jessica's throat. Imagination supplied a picture of Karl, wielding a hairbrush, trying to tie a slippery satin ribbon into a bow.

"It's a bit loose." Jessica's fingers trembled as she retied the bow.

Molly was very quiet as they walked to the hospital. On the maternity floor Jessica stopped by the foyer.

"You go on ahead. I'll be along in five minutes."

Karl didn't argue. He just put an arm around her shoulders and hugged her to his side. "No." His tone cut off all protests. "You're coming with us."

At the door of his sister's private room, he stopped, letting Molly go ahead.

"Mommy?" There was uncertainty on the girl's face as she looked at her mother in the hospital bed, surrounded by unfamiliar equipment.

"Darling!" Andy Spencer's face glowed with love as she opened her arms to her firstborn.

Andy was so beautiful. Silky blond hair like her daughter's, and even from this distance, Jessica could tell her eyes would be just like Karl's. She wore a pink bed-jacket over her hospital gown.

"Oh, Mommy, I was scared...." Jim Spencer rescued the pot of violets just in time as Molly went into her mother's arms.

Jessica blinked rapidly. Her glasses were getting steamed up again.

Jim Spencer came toward them, shook Jessica's hand and said, "Jessica, I'm Jim. Glad to meet you."

With an arm around Molly, Andy held her hand out to Jessica. "Jessica, I'm so glad you could come. Thank you for everything."

Jessica didn't quite know why she ended up hugging Andy, but she did. It had something to do with the warmth in the dark eyes so like Karl's, the sheen of moisture in her own.

"Mommy, does it hurt?" Molly's eyes were on the intravenous bag of saline suspended by her mother's bed, the tubes that connected her to it.

"Not anymore." Over her daughter's head, her gaze locked with her husband's. The look they exchanged proclaimed it had all been worth it.

"When can I see the baby?" Molly demanded.

"I'll take you right now." Jim Spencer put a hand out to his daughter, and they left the room hand in hand.

"Everything all right, Sis?" Karl came up the other side and ran a hand over his sister's head.

"I'm so happy, K." Andy turned her head so that her cheek rested briefly in her brother's palm. The diminutive she used emphasized their closeness.

"Richard Karl is doing so well in his incubator. Everything's turned out fine. Thank you both—" she included Jessica in her warm smile "—for all you've done for us."

"Isn't that what families are for?" Karl demanded.

Andy rested against her pillows. For an instant, as Andy looked at her brother, Jessica saw pain in both their eyes. It wasn't hard to guess they were both thinking of their parents.

"I called Mother and Dad this morning," Andy said carefully.

"How are they?"

"They're fine." Andy picked up the pot of violets and buried her face in it. "Said they'll be here in July. They're planning a cruise to the Bahamas then."

"I see."

This was late February. Andy's wording made it seem as if seeing Richard Karl was secondary to the senior Wagner's cruise.

Jessica's heart contracted with pain as she looked at their faces. Emotional wounds rarely healed completely. Time just covered them with a thin shield.

Andy turned to Jessica, obviously wanting to change the subject. "Molly hasn't stopped talking about you since the day you met. Tell me about your family. I always wanted a large family, but Jim says he's leaving home if I ever mention the subject again."

They laughed and talked till Jim returned with Molly.

"Before you go," Jim said, his tone indicating visiting hours were over, "Molly and I have something for you, Andy."

"I have everything I want." The sparkle in Andy's eyes was a sharp contrast to the pallor of her face.

The box Jim drew out of his pocket was wrapped in silver foil. Andy handed it to Molly to unwrap, saying her fingers were weak with excitement. Taking the jeweler's box Molly held out to her, Andy flipped the lid back.

"You shouldn't have. Not now, when we have all these pills to pay." The tears in her eyes as she looked at her husband, his answering look as he moved to take her in his arms, sealed them off in a world of their own.

"Oh, yes, I should have." He pressed his lips against her hair.

Andy held the box out to the others and concentrated on kissing her husband. Nestling on a bed of olive green velvet was an incredibly intricate gold bracelet set with the tiniest pearls Jessica had ever seen, and midnight blue sapphires.

Molly picked up the bracelet and handed it to her mother. "Look inside," she commanded.

Andy read the inscription out loud. "Richard Karl." It was followed by the date.

"It's beautiful."

"Mommy has another bracelet with my name inside it," Molly told Jessica proudly. "Daddy gave her that one when I was born."

Karl pulled something out of the pocket of his jeans.

"Another present?" Andy's eyebrows threatened to disappear into her hairline. "You've already offered to pay to have the baby's room decorated in the new house."

"That's for Richard Karl," said her brother. "This is for you."

It was a pendant to match the bracelet. Karl and Andy's husband must have shopped together. Heart-shaped, the pendant featured pearls and sapphires that caught the light and glittered.

"You spend too much money on us," Andy reproved Karl.

"What's it there for, anyway?" A shrug dismissed the cost of the gift, his sister's thanks.

A look passed between Jim and Karl, and the latter got to his feet. Andy was definitely looking worn-out.

"Time to go," Karl said, pretending to stifle a yawn. "Bet everyone's going to be glad of an early night tonight."

Molly kissed her mother and her father. Though Andy looked tired, she protested their leaving and urged them to come early the next day.

"Jessica, thank you for coming and for the port-a-crib. I wanted one of those. Come visit us soon, in our new house."

"I will," Jessica promised, and then they were all being ushered out by a determined Jim.

They stopped off at the nursery. Richard Karl was in an incubator that had been moved near the large window so they could see him easily.

Molly pressed her nose to the glass again. "Mommy touched him this morning," she said. "There's a special place in the incubator she can put her hand through. Daddy says it's important for babies to be held. They need to feel they're loved."

Jessica looked at Molly's little brother, and her throat closed up. He looked like a crumpled rose, eyes closed, hands curled into fists.

"Daddy says I looked just like Rikki when I was born."

"Rikki?" her uncle questioned.

"It's what I'm going to call him," Molly explained. "He looks just like Rikki Tikki Tavi."

Jessica's mouth worked. The baby looked just like Rudyard Kipling's mongoose? She dared not look at Karl. The baby was so beautiful. Perfect in every detail. Jessica thought of the physical and mental strain Andy had undergone to have her son. Yet today she looked ready to do it all over again. Jessica blinked. The miracle of motherhood was one of the most moving.

A touch on her shoulder made Jessica start.

"Penny for them?"

"My mother says a child is a man and a woman's gift to the world. A sign of their belief in the future. Belief that there will be a world of peace and happiness for that child to live and grow in."

Karl's hand tightened on her shoulder. Jessica stole a glance upward. There was an amazing softness on his face. "I'd like to meet your mother sometime."

"She'd like to meet you, too." Suddenly it seemed important to let him know the comment didn't signify anything deeper. "Our house is always full of friends and family. Visitors say they've stopped trying to sort out the relatives from the rest. It's easier that way."

Karl smiled, then turned as Molly tugged at his sleeve. "Uncle Karl, what are we going to have for dinner? I'm starving."

"Give me a minute, Molly, and I'll think of something." He turned to Jessica. "Want to come eat with us?"

Jessica looked at him and shook her head. "No, thanks. I have a few errands to run."

The way she felt, she needed a little time to herself.

Karl hesitated, then nodded. "Talk to you tomorrow, then."

"Tomorrow," echoed Jessica.

They parted at her car. She drove home feeling lonely and teary, wondering if she was coming down with the flu.

About to attribute it to lack of sleep, Jessica paused. She'd never lied to herself and didn't intend starting now. Her moodiness had something to do with the way Jim Spencer had looked at his wife. Jessica knew she wanted someone to look at her like that.

She took a deep breath. Not just anyone. Karl.

The way Karl had looked at the baby was branded on her mind. Wistful, longing, *needing*. It wasn't the look of a man who was content to remain single. It was the look of a man who didn't dare reach out for what he wanted because he didn't want to hurt another human being as his mother had been hurt.

She didn't know a single other man who thought like him. She knew so many who took what they wanted without consideration for anyone's feelings but their own.

Jessica pulled into the covered parking space by her apartment and put her head on the steering wheel for a second.

Convincing Karl Wagner he would make an idea husband and father made the labors of Hercules seem like child's play.

"Balance it on the tip of your finger, squeeze the solution onto it, hold your eye open with one hand and flip it into place. There you go! Now, think positive thoughts," Jessica ordered her reflection. "The new contacts are going to do just fine in your eyes. You are not going to have any problem with them. Wearing them is just a question of mind over matter."

Dr. Phillips, her optometrist, had been very positive about the latest pair of contact lenses. "Everyone whom

I've recommended them to has done very well with them,"
he'd told her. "They're especially made for sensitive eyes."

Jessica stood back. The contacts did make a difference to
her face. Without the glasses her eyes looked bigger, her
mouth less full. She smoothed down the tangerine pants she
had on. The olive green top and matching jacket went well
with it. Yes, she actually looked nice for a change.

The Spencers had invited her to dinner tonight. Andy had
been home with the baby three weeks now. Arthur had been
taken over to the new house a fortnight ago. Molly called
every other day with glowing reports of Arthur and the new
baby, her Nana and Gramps. Uncle Karl, she'd reported,
had gone to the Midwest for a week. A dental conference.

Jessica had assured herself she didn't mind in the least
where he went. He hadn't contacted her after the day she'd
visited Andy in the hospital, and Jessica had let it be. Rome
hadn't been built in a day, and neither was any lasting relationship. But the thought that he had left Clearview ran-
kled.

Karl Wagner didn't have to call and let her know he was
leaving town. He didn't have to call and let her know if he
was leaving the country. Repeating the thought to herself as
she ate her way through two pounds of chocolates, removed her artificial nails and chewed on her real ones till the
skin at the tips of her fingers began to smart, hadn't helped.
Telling herself he wasn't the only fish in the ocean didn't do
her any good, either. He was the only fish she wanted.

Picking up her bag, Jessica turned to leave the apartment, telling herself she was getting over Karl Wagner really
well. He could move to Timbuktu, for all she cared.

Jim and Molly greeted her at the door of their new home
in Walnut.

"How are you, Jessica?" Jim looked relaxed and happy.

"Come, see the baby," Molly said as she dragged Jessica into the living room.

Behind them, Jim chuckled and said, "I have my work cut out getting attention around here these days." His happiness proclaimed he didn't want it any other way.

"It's good to see you again, Jessica," Andy said, smiling warmly at her over the water-filled baby bottle she was holding. "How have you been?"

"Fine, thanks. Busy at work." Jessica moved to stand behind Andy so she could look down at Rikki. Something warned her that Andy knew how she felt about Karl, and Jessica didn't want pity.

The baby's eyes were open, and he was staring straight at her as he drank the water. "Hi, Rikki," she said softly.

"He's doing so well," said Andy proudly. "Gaining weight steadily and hardly ever cries."

Jim reached for the baby, placed him on his shoulder and burped him.

"Jessica, meet my parents." He smiled at the older couple who had just come downstairs. "Richard and Marina Spencer. Jessica Hansen."

The Spencers smiled and shook hands. "Karl has told us so much about you."

Karl? Surely they meant Molly? Jessica's smile froze.

"Did you have a pleasant flight out?" Jessica asked. A change of subject was called for.

"Yes, thank you. We hoped to be here before the baby arrived, but this young man had his own plans." Marina Spencer beamed fondly at her grandson.

"Just like his mother and sister," interjected Jim. "It's a good thing I'm easygoing. Three strong-willed people are enough for one man to have to cope with."

"Except," contributed his father with a straight face, "that under the so-called easygoing exterior is a will as strong as iron. When one comes up against that, it takes more than three people to turn you around, son."

"Dad! We men are supposed to stick together," Jim protested.

"Thanks, Richard." Andy chuckled gleefully.

"I just have to check on the roast a minute," Jim's mother excused herself. "We're having a real English dinner tonight. Yorkshire pudding and roast beef."

"I'm not much of a cook," confessed Andy. "Marina always takes over the kitchen when she's here. It makes it all the harder when she leaves."

Marina smiled comfortingly. "It'll come in time, dear. When Richard and I got married, I remember once boiling an egg for thirty minutes."

The older woman moved toward the kitchen, and Jessica went with her.

"May I help you in here?" Her eyes were beginning to smart. So much for willpower and the new contacts. "Not really dear, thank you." Marina Spencer smiled sweetly at her. "There's someone out there who wants to meet you, I think."

Jessica looked at the kitchen window. Arthur had his paws on the wooden ledge outside and was watching her, his body wriggling with excitement.

"I'll just say hello," Jessica said with a laugh.

"Hi, there, fella." She rubbed the back of Arthur's neck. "I missed you. Do you like your new home?"

She looked around. The Spencers had a large yard with a couple of huge trees and a nine-by-six wooden storage shed. She could make out the name Arthur painted on the top in block letters. A perfect dog house for someone his size. She knew he was going to be very happy here. He had so many people to keep him company now.

Jessica wondered who was keeping Karl company these days. If he missed Arthur at all. Missed *her*.

Chapter Eight

"Hello, Jessica."

She stiffened, then turned slowly. Karl stood just outside the patio door, his silhouette outlined in gold by the light from the house.

The first spurt of joy was replaced by anger. Why wasn't he in the Midwest raking defenseless women with that glance of his, reducing them to boneless heaps of helplessness?

"Hello, Karl."

"How have you been?"

"Fine, thanks." *As if he cared.* "And you?"

Darkness was a friend, providing cover, providing space. Electricity was a force flashing between them, drawing her inevitably toward him. It was as if their time apart had never been. Jessica clung to Arthur's collar.

"The conference was interesting, but I'd rather have stayed here."

Don't let that honey seep into your bones. His on-again, off-again manner has nothing to recommend it.

Fury kept her quiet.

"Didn't you get my message? A colleague who was presenting a paper met with an accident, and I was asked to fill in for him at the last minute." Karl's voice held traces of puzzlement.

"Message?" said Jessica blankly. If he thought Molly telling her he was away was a message, he had another think coming.

Even in the dark she could hear the change of tone. "Didn't Mrs. Lucas call you?"

"No," Jessica said coldly. "It doesn't matter. Molly told me you were on a business trip."

"Of course it matters...."

"It's nice out here, isn't it?" Drink in hand, Richard Spencer joined them on the patio. Unaware of interrupting anything, Richard said easily, "Jessica, Jim's wondering what you would like to drink."

Mumbling something about orange juice, Jessica slipped inside. She headed straight for the rest room. Her eyes were beginning to redden. If she removed the contacts, she would trip over her own toes. As part of her positive-thinking routine, she hadn't brought her glasses along. Wanting to be and making an effort didn't always add up to success.

Just a little while more, please, she prayed before joining the others in the living room.

Jim handed her a glass of orange juice.

"Jessica, want to look at my baby pictures?" Molly asked, looking up from the open album on her lap.

"I think Jessica was out on the patio with Uncle Karl," Andy intervened. "Maybe she would like to go back outside."

"No, that's all right. I just wanted to say hello to Arthur." Jessica smiled vaguely at Andy, hoping she'd leave it at that as she sat down beside Molly. "I'd like to look at your pictures, Molly."

Karl and Richard Spencer came in when Marina summoned everyone to dinner. Karl looked at Jessica as they all sat down in the formal dining room, and he frowned. "Where are your glasses?"

So much for stunning the world with her newly unveiled beauty.

"I'm wearing contacts," Jessica said coolly, resisting the temptation to blink rapidly and expel the irritating objects from her eyes.

"I see."

Andy had seated them across from each other at the table. Jessica refused to look at Karl. She concentrated on talking to Richard and Jim Spencer, aware all the while of Karl's gaze on her. Her eyes were beginning to burn. As soon as she'd helped wash up, she was going to have to leave.

"Know what Arthur did yesterday, Jessica?"

Jessica looked at Molly seated between her uncle and grandmother. "Nothing bad, I hope."

Molly grinned. "Nana and I helped Mommy take Rikki to the doctor for his checkup after I got home from school. Arthur got into our neighbor's yard. They had a portable clothesline outside, and the clothes were flapping in the breeze. Arthur thought it was a game of some sort and started barking and jumping at the clothes. Gramps heard him and rushed outside, but by then the clothesline had been knocked over and Arthur had Mr. O'Connor's blue spotted boxer shorts over his head. Arthur couldn't understand why it was so dark all of a sudden. He kept pawing at the shorts and whining. As soon as Gramps pulled them off Arthur's head, he ran for home as if he was being chased. He hasn't been near the fence since."

Jessica joined in the general laughter, but kept her eyes on her plate. Karl was still staring at her. Hadn't someone told him about trespassing on personal space?

"It *was* funny," Andy agreed, "but we're lucky the O'Connors weren't upset. They love dogs, it seems, but Mrs. O'Connor's allergies won't allow them to have one at home."

"Gramps helped Mrs. O'Connor pick up all her laundry," Molly continued. "I think Arthur kind of knew he'd done something bad, because he was awfully quiet the rest of the day."

"How was the conference, Karl?" Andy asked her brother. "You must be tired, coming straight here from the airport."

"Not really. I wanted to see—" the pause had a pulse leap into life in Jessica's throat "—you all. Coming here is better than going back to an empty house."

"A sure sign that your bachelor days are almost over, my friend," teased Jim. "Weren't you the one that said you liked being on your own after a busy day at the clinic?"

Under cover of the others' conversation Jessica went over what Karl had said. He missed Arthur. That was the only logical reason for his remarks.

"Mother, leave the dishes," Jim commanded as his mother stood up to remove the dessert plates. "Dad and I are going to take care of them later. Thank you for the delicious meal."

"Marina, that was heavenly," Andy seconded. "I'm going to put on a ton, but the good part is I don't even care. It's all Jim's fault. He says he loves me, no matter what I look like."

The look she exchanged with her husband was what Jessica called a bedroom look. It made everyone else feel superfluous.

"I could give you a hand with the dishes, Jim," offered Andy.

"No, you won't," he said firmly. "I have my orders from Dr. Ahmed. He let you out of the hospital early because you insisted on it, but if you don't rest till he gives the all clear, I'm going to have him readmit you."

"I'm getting awfully spoiled," protested Andy.

"Just remember this when it's Wimbledon time and I'm glued to the television," Jim said with a laugh.

Jessica was feeling oddly nervous. Karl's gaze seemed to have been glued to her face for the past few minutes. He set his napkin down and rose. "If you will all excuse us, Jessica and I have to leave now."

Jessica blinked. The surprise on her face was mirrored on everyone else's. Karl came around the table, cupped her elbow in the palm of his hand. A jolt racked Jessica. "Thank you for a wonderful dinner, Marina," Karl said politely. "Richard, I'll let you know about the days we can play golf. Good night, everybody. Please excuse us for running out on you. Andy, I'll call you tomorrow."

Jessica found she was being propelled away from the table. She barely managed a thank-you before she was hustled out of the room.

Karl put her into her car and shut the door. "I'll follow you home."

Jessica's heart was pounding too loudly for her to think. Random thoughts flung themselves at her. What on earth was the matter with Karl? How on earth was she ever going to face the Spencer family again? How dare Karl strong-arm her?

Jessica convinced herself she was angry by the time she parked her car and reached her front door. The irregularity of her heartbeat hinted at excitement, not anger.

Karl followed her in and kicked the door shut. The sound made Jessica jump.

"What on earth's wrong with you?" she demanded. She'd never seen him so furious.

"Not me. You." The clipped tones held no further clue. "Get those contacts out before they damage your eyes."

Jessica stared at him, opened her mouth, then closed it again. So that was what this was all about. Spinning on her heel, she went into the bathroom and shut the door with a bang.

Slipping the contacts out provided instant relief.

"That's better." Karl turned to her as soon as she entered the room.

The tension lifted off his face. One would think he'd been the one suffering. Jessica stayed silent. She couldn't trust herself to speak. For what she had to say to Karl Wagner, she needed calm, cool, collected. It was the only way to annihilate his take-charge tactics once and for all.

"Let me look at your eyes."

A hand lifted her chin while the other took her glasses off. Then both palms cupped her face. He frowned as he looked at her eyes. "Why on earth did you have to go and use contacts? Your eyes are definitely too sensitive for them."

Enough was enough. Thumping heart or not, Jessica wrenched away from him and crossed to the window. With her back to it, she folded her arms across her chest. Sparks shot out of her eyes as she sent him an icy glare. "That's none of your business."

He wasn't one to take a hint easily. "Why, Jessica? Why put yourself through so much misery?"

Tears of rage crept into her throat. "Because I'm sick of wearing glasses, that's why... because I don't like the way I look in them... because I want to look different."

She looked down at her feet. Suddenly there was no anger left. Only the pain of humiliation. Not for a million dollars would she cry in front of Karl.

"What's wrong with the way you look?" The surprise in his voice came through clearly.

Jessica turned to the window, made a show of pulling the drapes open. There was nothing to look at outside except the darkness.

"You won't understand," she said bitterly. "You've got enough good looks for two men."

There. It's out now. Let's see how he likes plain speaking.

"That's what this is all about? The way you look?"

Jessica stared out of the window in stubborn silence. His reflection moved in the clear glass . . . came toward her. Jessica spun around.

He didn't look scornful. The expression in his eyes was indefinable. Soft, understanding, *tender*. She stopped breathing.

He lifted his hands and threaded them through her hair, fingers splayed. His thumbs drew whorls of comfort on her temples as her face tilted to his.

"Jessica, listen to me," he ordered sternly. "You *are* beautiful. I thought so from the day I saw you in the mall." He watched the rigidity on her face remain unchanged. "Beauty isn't the way you look or your vital statistics. It's caring about things, about people. Wanting to change what's wrong even if it means going out on a limb. Having enough room in your heart for the whole world. It's the ability to give without counting the cost."

The look in his eyes burned a path to her brain. His words followed and imprinted themselves there. "Traits like yours can never be bought or bottled, Jessica. They spring from within you." He bent and touched his lips to hers in a brief salute. "Your kind of beauty is very rare, very unique. Soul-deep, not skin-deep."

Till she woke up, she intended enjoying every moment of this dream. Karl's voice held so much conviction, Jessica was ready to be teamed against Cleopatra and Helen of Troy. As soon as she got over her shock, that is.

Karl looked at the expression of wonder on her face, the lingering incredulity.

"Believe it, sweetheart." His whisper fled into her mouth as their lips met again.

There wasn't any way she could hold back her response. If Karl insisted on slaying her dragons, he had to take the consequences. Jessica clung to him, returning his kisses with fervor. She'd missed him so much. As he deepened the kisses, she let her hands roam his back, explore the muscles in his shoulders.

"Jessica." He caught hold of her hands and brought them to his chest. The fact that he was out of breath, as bemused as she was, made Jessica feel even more wonderful.

"It's time I was leaving." Karl looked away from her as he spoke.

Jessica blinked. The words shredded her happiness. Karl was doing that odd dance-step again. One forward. Two back.

At the look on her face, Karl crushed her to him again and growled, "Jessica, I don't want to hurt you. Ever."

He wasn't running away for his sake. He was running for hers. Jessica shut her eyes as the truth surfaced.

Karl...who could transform a plain Jane into Aphrodite, who could replace fear with courage, who could love without asking for love in return, still didn't trust himself in a close relationship.

Jessica put her hands against his chest and pushed away from him. "Karl Wagner—" she tilted her head and looked him straight in the eye "—you may not have noticed it, but I'm all grown-up. I can take care of myself. If you're backing out of this because you don't *want* to go on, that's different. If you're backing out because you're afraid of the pain you think you'll cause me, think again. I'm little but I'm strong."

He stared at her as if he could devour her with his gaze. Jessica's heart was doing cymbal clashes, but she wasn't going to stop now. Stepping closer, she framed his face with her hands. "Now, where were we when you interrupted?"

For one heart-stopping moment, she thought he wouldn't lean down to her. But he did. Jessica's eyes closed in thankfulness as their lips meshed.

So far, so good. They had reached a plateau of understanding. The rest of the climb would have to be done in careful stages. They had quite a way to go before the summit.

The first thing Jessica did the next morning was throw her contacts away.

"Jessica, I'm so glad you could come," Andy said with a smile. From the back of the Spencer's house, deep barks underlined her welcome. "Richard and Marina have taken Molly shopping, so it's just the two of us and Rikki for a while."

"How is Rikki?" The name suited the baby, with his big brown eyes.

"Just look at him," Andy said. He lay asleep in his mother's arms, the picture of contented infancy. "He's growing so fast even the doctor's surprised."

"I'll just say hello to Arthur and be right back."

Greetings completed, she went to wash her hands. The powder room brought back memories of her last visit here and Karl's reaction. He hadn't contacted her since last Saturday. The week had dragged by interminably. When Andy had called yesterday to invite Jessica to lunch, she hadn't mentioned her brother. Neither had Jessica.

Practicing patience was an art she hadn't cultivated. Doing so now was very hard, but she was going to let Karl make the next move.

Jessica dried her hands and rejoined Andy in the family room.

"Here, want to hold him?" Andy offered. Rikki was awake, his dark eyes scanning everything around him.

He fitted just right in the crook of her arm. Rikki grinned as she whispered a soft hello. Jessica's heart contracted. She didn't care if cynics said babies' smiles were just caused by air. She preferred to think they were real.

"Hi, sweetheart!" she greeted him softly. There was fuzz on the top of his head now, and the nails at the end of his clenched fists looked long.

Andy poured two cups of coffee and brought one to Jessica, who set it on an end table.

"I'm so lucky," Andy said, staring thoughtfully at her son. "Not a day goes by that I don't wake up and give thanks for everything." She sipped her coffee and then said slowly, "When I think of myself a few years back, how life would have turned out if I hadn't met Jim...." Andy shuddered. "He turned my life around."

"How did you and Jim meet?" Maybe she could learn something more about Karl, understand him better, by listening to his sister.

"I was in New York with a crowd that was up to no good. I had no money, no ambition. Every day was a blur. One day I was out on the street, mingling with the rush hour crowd, trying to find someone whose pocket I could pick. I didn't know Jim had spotted me. As I closed into my victim, Jim shackled my wrist, saying, 'Not today, you don't.'"

"And then?" Television, thought Jessica, should be so interesting.

"He took me to a park and talked to me for hours. Asked me if I knew what the consequences were." Jessica's mind instantly replayed her encounter with the two miscreants at the plaza and Karl's leniency with them. She understood the reason for it so much better now. "Jim asked me about my family. I refused to tell him anything. He took me to a fast-food place, bought me all the food I could eat and told me if I wanted another good meal, I had to meet him in the same spot the next day. And that's how it began. The reformation of Andy Wagner." Andy laughed, but the tears weren't far away. "It took a long while, though, for me to believe in love, to give myself a chance. Karl's the same." Taking the sleeping baby from Jessica, she held him close, as if to chase the blackness of her memories away. "I'll put him in his port-a-crib. He's getting too used to being held all day long."

Jessica picked up her mug and sipped her coffee thoughtfully. Andy had slipped the advice into her conversation so casually, yet Jessica knew what Karl's sister was trying to tell her. Mental and emotional wounds sometimes took longer to heal than physical ones.

"I was always the rebellious one at home," Andy said, sitting down again and picking up her coffee cup. "I threw tantrums, I ran away from home, I let my parents know what I thought of them. Karl just kept quiet and slipped away to college." She sipped her coffee, her eyes dark with the pain of memories. "Karl was always there for me when we were growing up. He'd spend hours talking to me. He'd take me shopping, to the movies. He tried so hard to talk some sense into me when I insisted on dating the worst boys in school. But I tuned him out as I searched for an escape from the mountain of pain inside me. It got worse after he went away to college. I stuck it out till I finished high school, and then I ran away. Karl gave up one semester of his dental studies to try and find me. He put notices in all the papers, followed every lead the police had on missing people. When Jim called him, he came to New York right away. I thought he'd be mad, but he just held me and tears filled his eyes. 'I'm sorry,' he kept saying. 'I'm sorry. I should never have left home.' The fact that he blamed himself, not me, made me realize how much he loved me. He never talks about the past now, but of the two of us, I think he was hurt most, because he never expressed his feelings like I did. Has he talked to you about it?"

"A bit."

"I've never seen him with anyone the way he was with you the night you both came to dinner. It was as if he was hurting as much as you were. It gave me hope. Was he very angry about the contacts?"

Jessica tried to laugh it off, though her heart accelerated at the memory of Karl's kisses. "No. He merely talked some sense into me that day."

Andy set her mug down and leaned forward. "Jessica, maybe I shouldn't say anything. Jim warned me about interfering, but I can't help myself. Karl's not like other men. He can't open up easily. He doesn't trust himself not to turn into the living image of my father."

"I know."

"If you really care about him, let your love—"

The family burst in, loaded down with parcels. To Jessica's surprise, Jim was right behind them. Andy had mentioned yesterday he had to work today.

"Jim!" Andy's face lit up as if she hadn't seen her husband for months. "I thought you weren't coming home till five."

"Hello, darling." Jim kissed her and then said, "Thought I'd spend the afternoon with my family. I looked out of the window at twelve and suddenly couldn't stand to be away from all of you a minute longer." He motioned to the files under his arm. "I can always work at night. That's one thing good about being a chartered accountant. You can take your work around with you." Placing an arm around his wife's shoulders, he smiled warmly at Jessica. "Hello, Jessica. It's good to see you again."

"Mommy, can I show Jessica the house now?" Molly asked when Andy moved to the kitchen to help her husband get lunch ready.

"Of course."

There were five bedrooms and a bonus room upstairs. Molly stopped in the doorway of the fifth bedroom. "This is the guest room," she announced. "Jessica, would you like to come and stay the weekend sometime? What with Rikki and Arthur and school, I won't see much of you otherwise."

"I'd love to come for the weekend," said Jessica warmly. "And you can come and spend a weekend with me, as well. I don't have an extra bedroom, but the couch in my living room pulls out to make a nice bed."

Happy, Molly nodded. "I'd like that. I don't think Arthur will mind if I leave him for one night. He's used to Mommy and Daddy and Nana and Gramps now. Mommy says Arthur thinks *he's* Rikki's full-time baby-sitter. When Rikki cries, Arthur goes looking for Mommy and nudges her with his nose."

Molly's conversation clued her in to the little girl's happiness. That her thoughts were never far from the dog she'd adopted was a sure sign how much she loved Arthur. Jessica was glad he'd fitted in so well.

As they went downstairs, Molly told her how Gramps had helped take Arthur to the vet on the weekend for his checkup, how Nana was going to teach her to knit.

The table was set in the kitchen. Jim carried a tuna salad to the table while Andy set out a platter of sandwich meat, cheese slices, a loaf of rye bread and peanut butter and jelly.

"Marina's planned steak-and-kidney pie for dinner to-night," Andy said to Jessica as they all sat down. "Would you like to stay for dinner?"

"No, thanks, Andy. I have to take some books back to the library before it closes at four, then my brother David's coming over for the rest of the weekend."

"Nana, do you know Jessica has six brothers and four sisters?" Molly asked her grandmother. "Eleven kids and their mother and father make thirteen. Do you have a very big house, Jessica?"

"My Mom tells me Dad added a room for every two kids, a bathroom for every three, so now we have seven bed-rooms, five bathrooms. The oldest boy and the oldest girl living at home had their own bedrooms, but the rest of us had to share, two to a room."

"It's a lovely day outside," Jim said later when there was a pause in the lunchtime conversation. "Want me to move Rikki's port-a-crib and an air mattress under the maple tree in the backyard?" he asked his wife. "You can have your nap out there."

"Why don't we all go to the beach," Andy suggested, looking around the table. "I haven't been to the ocean for ages. It's such a nice day. There'd be plenty of room for everyone if we took the van."

No one seconded her. Jessica could tell from the island of silence that Andy wasn't on the completely well list yet.

It was Jim who finally broke the silence. "Not yet, Andy. Not till the doctor says you can."

"Oh, but Jim..." Andy began, only to be silenced by the look in her husband's eyes. He just held her gaze quietly. Instead of anger Jessica sensed the love in his glance, the soft understanding in his eyes as he looked at his wife.

"Not yet, Andy," he repeated without changing his tone.

Jessica tensed for battle. Nothing about Andy Spencer suggested meekness. This was one woman who would never accept dominance.

"Oh, okay, you old fussbudget." The fact there was no rancor in Andy's tone amazed Jessica. Jumping up from her chair, Andy sat down on her husband's lap and twined her arms around his neck. The kiss she gave him was very, very thorough.

Jim's eyes were glinting when she got off his lap and marched into the kitchen.

"Minx!" was all he said under his breath.

When it was time to leave, Andy kissed Jessica on the cheek and said, "Forgive me for interfering? Jim and Karl would both have my hide if they knew I was meddling in your affairs."

Jessica smiled through sudden tears. No one knew better than she did that caring, real caring, was reason enough to interfere. "I'm glad we could talk."

Back in her apartment Jessica kicked off her shoes and flung herself down on her bed. She had a lot of thinking to do.

Life wasn't a set of rules that never changed. Life was constant change, constant exchange.

Karl was silly to think he would turn into his father. Each generation was molded by different circumstances, different influences. Surely he knew just the conscious will to change would prevent him from being a cold partner. Why did he have to hold on to his fears so tenaciously?

*Just the way you hold onto the thought marriage means
being dominated.*

Jessica blinked. Her mouth dropped open. She was guilty
as charged.

The idea that marriage automatically meant being dominated wasn't true. Dominance alone was certainly not to be
tolerated, but dominance stemming from love and concern
was something entirely different. It wasn't even dominance
then; it was just a looking out for the other person. Jim and
Andy had offered proof of that today.

Jessica was beginning to understand some things more
clearly now. She saw her sisters' choices in a different light.
Everyone adapted the age-old pattern of marriage and life
to suit their own personal preferences. What looked like a
willingness to be dominated to an outsider was really just a
matter of choices.

Jessica had chosen, too. She wanted Karl.

The thing was getting him to acknowledge the fact that
they were made for each other.

"Karl?" The silence at the other end made Jessica's heart
hammer against her ribs. She shouldn't have called him.

"Jessica, how are you?" His tone didn't give anything
away.

"I'm fine." She blinked rapidly and tightened her grip on
the receiver. "I was wondering if you would like to come to
my place for dinner Friday night?"

She closed her eyes. She wasn't being too forward, she
told herself fiercely, it was just helping things along.

"Friday?" He sounded surprised.

"Yes." The well of babbling she could always tap into
had dried up. Even the monosyllable she'd just uttered
seemed superfluous. "I've had so many meals at your place.
It's time I returned the hospitality."

"What time would you like me to come over?"

He'd said *yes*? Jessica held the receiver away from her ear and stared at it just to be sure.

"Seven?"

"See you then, Jessica." The soft click told her he wasn't on the line any longer.

On the plus side was the fact he hadn't refused. On the minus side was the fact he hadn't exactly jumped for joy.

Why on earth had she gone against the deeply ingrained principle that a man had to do the chasing? Watching a commercial that said it was okay for a woman to call the shots was very different from actually doing it. Jessica blinked. Friday was five days away. She still had time to call him and cancel. But she wouldn't.

Her doorbell rang at five minutes after seven, Friday night. Jessica took a deep breath, patted the cowl neck of her aquamarine blue dress and wished herself luck as she went to the door.

"Karl, how are you?"

He stood before her, freshly showered, dressed in navy blue slacks and a white shirt. Jessica's hand tightened on the doorknob so she wouldn't throw herself at him.

"Good evening, Jessica." The half smile he gave her didn't reveal anything of his feelings. He would make a great poker player.

He came into the room and held out a bunch of carnations, dyed pale peach.

"Thank you, Karl." Jessica's fingers trembled as she took the flowers from him. They hadn't been in the same room five minutes, and already the air crackled with tension. She desperately searched for a light, witty remark that would defuse it.

"The flowers reminded me of your skin." Karl was giving her that intent look of his. His eyes were laced with a new expression she couldn't understand. Pain? Jessica's heart spasmed at the thought of Karl in pain.

Her brain was atrophying, and the air supply to her lungs seemed to have been turned off. Had he said the delicate hue of the flowers reminded him of her skin?

"Shall I put them in water for you?" Karl asked.

Jessica collected herself. "No. No, thank you. I'll take care of them. Please sit down."

In her tiny kitchen Jessica stuffed the flowers into a glass filled with water and promised them better treatment later. Taking a deep breath, she rejoined Karl.

"What would you like to drink? I have Scotch and some California wine."

"I'll have some wine."

Filling two wine glasses carefully, Jessica arranged a bowl of nuts and a plate of vegetables and dip on the tray. Her hands shook, and twice she almost dropped something. It was worse than anything she'd ever anticipated.

Please help me get through this evening. I'll never again attempt something like this. Never.

There were women who could and women who couldn't. Take the initiative, that is. She definitely belonged in the latter category.

"Have you been very busy?" Jessica sat across from Karl.

"Kind of." She didn't miss the hesitation before he said, "Mrs. Lucas has had the flu, and the office is always chaotic when she's away."

"She called me last week and apologized for not giving me your message. Her sister being involved in that car accident must have been very upsetting for her. She said she rushed to the hospital, and for the next few days everything went out of her head except being with her sister."

Karl nodded. "She told me she called you and apologized."

"She did. She's such a nice person. There's something about her that cheers one up, just to look at her or talk to her."

Karl smiled. "Yes. I'm glad I went with my instinct and hired her. She's excellent with the kids and nervous parents, reliable and rarely misses a day of work. I wish I could say the same for all my staff."

Why were they doing this to each other? Jessica wondered miserably. Talking of everything and everyone, avoiding the real issue. Was it so hard to discuss how they felt about each other? A great sadness washed over her. She couldn't really force Karl into acknowledging his feelings. Love was a powerful motivator. If he cared enough, nothing would hold him back.

"Excuse me while I check on dinner," she said politely.

"Can I give you a hand with anything?" Two strangers couldn't have been more formal.

"No, thanks. Everything's under control."

Jessica longed for the old Karl. Warm, loving, *caring*. Was this new front a part of his plan to prove he was a cold person? She checked the barbecued chicken and the pasta salad she had picked up from the local deli after work.

They talked of Molly and Arthur while they ate, and of Jim's parents and Rikki.

"That was delicious." The fact that he'd taken very small helpings of everything didn't color Karl's praise. "Let me help clean up."

"No." Anger had a strong grip on Jessica. If he insisted on this cold formality between them, he was going to be treated like a stranger. "I'll take care of the dishes."

Karl raised his brow at her tone. "Something wrong?"

"Of course not," snapped Jessica as she piled everything recklessly on top of each other. "What could be wrong? It's been a perfect evening so far. Perfect conversation, a perfect dinner with a perfect guest."

His hand closed over hers. "When did you go back to biting your nails?"

Jessica looked from Karl to her hands, and rage sizzled to the surface. What right did he have to comment on her nails after treating her like a stranger all evening? She'd chew whatever she pleased.

"What's wrong, Jessica?"

"Nothing's wrong." Except the fact that she'd worn herself out, but the rock on his shoulder hadn't budged the tiniest bit. Jessica tried a laugh to back up her statement. It cracked in the middle. The ensuing silence ricocheted off the walls, closed in on her. Jessica set the pile of dishes down and abruptly pressed the back of her hand against her forehead. "I think you should leave now, before I say something I'll regret."

"Jessica." Karl stood up, reached for her.

She backed away, her color high, her eyes shooting sparks at him. "Please leave, Karl. I thought if we talked, you might see reason, but that's before I saw the way you were tonight. Stubborn, unbending, *mulish*. If you don't care enough to give yourself a chance, all the words in the world won't make a difference to you."

As the door closed behind Karl, Jessica realized she'd been so busy saying all the wrong things that all the right things she'd rehearsed all week long had been left unsaid.

Abandoning the idea of cleaning up, she burst into tears.

Chapter Nine

Jessica was angry. Not the quick flare that she usually experienced. That dwindled fast. This was a slow, steady burn, fueled by thoughts of Karl. The more she thought of the way he'd been Friday night, the angrier she became.

A mule could take lessons from Karl Wagner.

He hadn't contacted her at all since that night. She'd thought of calling and apologizing for saying he was stubborn and unbending. But then she knew if she called him, it would only be to add blind and obdurate to her list. The hope that something she'd said that night would have made a difference had died long ago.

In the past week Molly had called often, and Andy had talked to her once and suggested she come over for dinner. Jessica had refused the invitation politely but firmly. She wasn't going to keep meeting Karl. If it was over, it was over, period. She didn't have the stretchability of elastic. Besides, it was as important to know when to admit defeat as it was to know when to go on.

"Something's the matter with Uncle Karl," Molly informed her when she called Saturday. "He's very quiet and doesn't come over much. Last weekend I asked if he would come over for the day, but he said he had a lot of catching up to do. Do you think now that the baby's here, he thinks I no longer care for him?"

Jessica had to bite back a smile. Trust Molly to worry on an adult level. "I don't think it's that. He probably did have a great deal of paperwork to catch up on because Mrs. Lucas has been out of the office."

"I heard Mommy say it sounded like a bad case of jitteritis to her. Do you know what that means?"

"I have no idea." But she did. There was jitteritis that everyone had at decision time, then there was Karl's variety. Chronic. The kind with no cure.

"Remember, you're spending next weekend with us," Molly reminded.

"I haven't forgotten," Jessica assured her. "Say hello to everyone for me."

"Know something, Jessica?" Molly was in no hurry to end the call. "The O'Connors said if there's a dog in the shelter that's not too hairy and won't shed much, they would like one. They said seeing Arthur made them decide they want one of their own very much. Mrs. O'Connor has talked to her doctor about it. The doctor told her that if she went to the shelter and got really close to the dog, she'd soon know if she was allergic to the animal or not. Do you think there's a dog for them at the shelter?"

"I'm going there this afternoon." Jessica had decided it was time to take José Garcia some of her chili. It always turned out well when she was angry. "I'll keep an eye out for a suitable dog."

Satisfied, Molly said goodbye and hung up.

Jessica stirred the chili, busy with her thoughts. That was two dogs she had to find today. Mrs. Lucas wanted a dog, as well. Karl's office manager had called her Monday at six and apologized all over again for not letting her have Karl's message. Jessica had known there had to be another reason behind the call, but she'd listened quietly as the office manager had told her her sister was recovering from the accident nicely. Mr. Lucas had the flu now, though, and to listen to the man carry on, you'd think the world was coming to an end.

"Jerry's been so difficult since he retired," she'd confided. "More demanding, easily offended and very moody. The doctor said it's a mild depression. Dr. Wagner suggested a dog might do him good. I was wondering if you could kind of pick one out for us? Not too big, because we have a small yard."

"I'd love to."

So Karl was back at it. Solving everyone else's problems and ignoring his own.

"Dr. Wagner said you'd know just the right dog for us. He says you have a knack for matching people with the right dog."

"Hmm."

She had a knack for matching Karl with the right person, too. If only he'd let go of his rock of insecurity.

"He's working much too hard these days," Mrs. Lucas offered, apropos of nothing.

"Oh?" Jessica had commented carefully.

"He's got something on his mind, for sure. Sits in that office for hours after everyone else has gone home. Says he has work to catch up with. Last week I forgot my bag in the office and had to go back for it. There he sat with his head in his hands and didn't even hear me come in."

Jessica threw in half a tin of chili powder into her chili a she recalled Mrs. Lucas's words. The thought of Karl alon and sad made her heart curl up in pain.

"Hmm." It wasn't brilliant. It was all she'd been capa ble of saying.

"I have to go now, dear. There's another call coming through. It's been so nice talking to you." Mrs. Lucas hac concluded hurriedly.

"I'll get back to you about the dog," Jessica hac promised.

She shook in some more chili powder, then frowned at the empty tin in her hands. Surely she hadn't emptied eigh ounces of chili powder in there? Oh well, she'd just warr José before he ate it.

Transferring a generous quantity of chili into a disposa ble container, Jessica picked up her car keys and set out fo the shelter earlier than she'd planned. She didn't want to b haunted by visions of Karl lonely and sad. All week she' thought of little else.

José was glad to see her. "How are you doing, Ms. Han sen, and how's the Great Dane?"

"He's the happiest dog in the world, José." Jessic beamed at the officer. "I'm sure there are days he wants t pinch himself to make sure he hasn't died and gone to do heaven."

"I'm so glad." He eyed the container she held in he hands. "Is that the chili you promised me?"

"It is. Good and hot," said Jessica cheerfully. "Peppe hot, not fire hot. Guaranteed to cause heartburn, gastro enteritis and an upset stomach."

"My stomach won't object. It's used to serrano and ja lapeño peppers," José said happily, his eyes glistening i anticipation of the meal.

"In that case you'll enjoy this," Jessica told him. "I've ut half a loaf of crusty French bread into the bag to go with . Mind if I look at the dogs while you eat?"

José looked a bit uneasy. "Are you sure that's a good lea?"

"Why not?" Surprise made Jessica quiz the expression on osé's face.

"Well…" José hitched his pants up with one hand. "You now what happened the last time you looked at them."

"But it all turned out fine, didn't it?" Jessica deanded.

"You were hurting so badly for that dog, I almost wanted take him home myself," José reminded her.

"What's wrong with caring?"

"Nothing," said José gently, "as long as it doesn't break our heart not to succeed."

Jessica thought about what José had said as she strolled etween the rows.

It was breaking her heart not to succeed with Karl. But if ove wasn't given unconditionally and without thought of elf, did it really qualify as love?

A black mongrel cringed as she approached his enclo- ire, shrinking into the farthest corner. His plume of a tail as tucked low, his bearing begged for mercy and his whole ody trembled.

"Who hurt you, sweetheart?" Jessica crooned softly. She ould see the Lucases with this dog, pampering him back to ust and love. He was just the right size, too. Once he'd re- vered his spirit, he would make a fine companion.

She remembered how Arthur had been the first time she'd sited him. Words wouldn't have convinced him then. Time nd actions proved points better than speeches.

Jessica's hands froze on the bar. That was it. Karl needed more than words to convince him of her love. He needed action.

"You want this one?" José's words floated to her on a wave of chili breath. He sounded gloomy.

"Wha...? No. I just had an idea."

"Oh?"

"Yes. Can you reserve this dog for me till tomorrow evening? And there's another one in that first row. Third from the right. A schnauzer. They don't shed, do they? I want him, too."

"Bought a house, have you?"

"What?" Jessica stared at him in surprise. "No, I haven't bought a house. You know I can't afford one. These two are for people I know. They'll stop by tomorrow to see the dogs."

"I'll put a hold on their cards, then."

Jessica flung her bag down on the couch as soon as she entered her apartment and dialed Karl's number. The receiver was lifted on the third ring.

"Karl, hi!"

"If you will leave your name and number, I will get back to you as soon as I can," intoned the answering machine.

She stared at the telephone receiver, frozen. An answering machine. He'd bought an answering machine. It was like a slap. He wanted to protect his privacy. He didn't want her calling and bothering him.

Her voice quivered as she left a message. "Karl, please call me."

He didn't return her call. Jessica called once a day for the next three days. Each time, she listened to the same message, left the same brief request.

As the week wore on, Jessica's anger escalated to volcanic proportions. By the time Molly called on Thursday, she was ready to erupt.

"Rikki's beginning to recognize me, Jessica," Molly announced. "He likes me to tickle his feet. Dr. Ahmed said Mommy's all better now, so Daddy's taking her out to dinner tonight. Nana and Gramps and I are going to take care of Rikki and have English fish and chips for dinner. Did you know the English like their ketchup mixed with vinegar? I do, too." The pause for breath didn't take long. "The O'Connors went to the shelter three times this week. Mrs. O'Connor's not allergic to schnauzers, so they're going to bring George home next week. Uncle Karl's in Mexico."

"Oh?" Jessica wondered if he was moving there to avoid her. The thought he hadn't returned her messages because he hadn't received them did make a difference, though.

"He's been helping at an American clinic that gives free dental aid to poor Mexicans. He does it once every year, for a week."

Drat the man. Why could she never stay angry with him?

"Nana and Gramps asked me if I would like to go to San Francisco for a week with them," continued Molly, unaware of the tidal waves of emotion her news created in Jessica's brain. "Miss Hedges, my teacher, says travel is an education in itself. Do you think Arthur will be very sad if I leave him?"

"No," said Jessica, her mind busy with pictures of Karl doing volunteer dental work in Mexico. Would that man ever slow down long enough to come to terms with his own needs? "He's going to miss you quite a bit, naturally, but he'll have your mommy and daddy to keep him company while you're gone."

"Rikki, too." The love Molly felt for her brother was obvious in her voice.

"Rikki, too," agreed Jessica, glad at how well everything had turned out for the Spencers.

Jessica called Mrs. Lucas the next day.

"I was wondering how you fared at the shelter?" she asked the older woman.

Mrs. Lucas had mentioned visiting the shelter with her husband on Wednesday. The clinic closed at twelve, and the staff had a half day off then.

"We liked the dog you picked," she said happily. "You should see Jerry with him. The dog makes him feel important and needed. It's the best medicine for him. He's more cheerful than I've seen him in a long while, spends a lot of time outdoors with Scrap and is even talking of taking him for walks."

Jessica stared at the telephone thoughtfully after the call. She'd had a great deal more to say to Mrs. Lucas, and all of it hadn't been to do with the dog.

"Is it okay if I go home early today?" Mrs. Lucas asked Karl his first day back. "I have a splitting headache."

"Sure." Karl nodded.

The last patient had just left five minutes ago. The four o'clock appointment had been canceled at the last minute, and his assistant had asked if she could leave early, as well. Karl was in his office putting a file away when Mrs. Lucas came in.

"Are you leaving now, too?" asked Mrs. Lucas.

"No," said Karl, wondering about the apprehensive look on his office manager's face. "I just want to go over a few of the patients' charts. I'll lock up when I leave."

He preferred the clinical surroundings of his office these days. At least here there were no reminders of a woman in an oversize bathrobe, with velvet lips and skin like silk. Of a face, tender, expressive, vulnerable, that haunted his every waking moment. Of eyes that simmered with pain while she accused him of being stubborn and unbending.

He was all that and more.

The emptiness inside had snowballed into a dark heap of despair. He'd thought the strenuous hours he'd worked in Mexico would fill the blanks in his life. Not so. At odd times he would think of her smile, the caring, and he would be overcome by the urge to return and tell her he loved her.

He wasn't sure when she had slipped past his guard. All he knew was she had reached a part of him no other woman had and that he didn't want to let go of her. Jessica was like a flower that relied on the warmth of the sun for life. He couldn't bear to risk thinking he might lessen her happiness in any way.

It was also why he hadn't made love to her. He didn't doubt the force of their desire or Jessica's willingness. But he couldn't simply take and not give. If he wasn't ready for heart-whole commitment, he had to protect her from their physical wish for a relationship. Someday she would meet someone else. If he couldn't be her husband, he didn't want to be a regret in her life, either.

He heard the outer door open and frowned. Mrs. Lucas always locked that one before she left. Maybe she'd forgotten something.

He peeped out of his office, and his heart did a quantum leap.

"Jessica! Is something wrong?" He was beside her instantly.

She was holding a hanky to her face. He caught the word, "...hurts."

"Your tooth hurts?"

Without waiting for her to say anything, he cupped her elbow, led her into the first treatment room and helped her into the shiny black chair. She hadn't removed the hanky from her face. Her eyes looked at him from behind her glasses, shining with trepidation.

Karl's heart contracted. He couldn't bear to see her in pain. He picked one hand up. Her pulse was rapid. He touched her forehead. She wasn't running a fever.

"There's nothing to be afraid of, Jessica," he said gently. Just looking at her filled the empty hole in his heart, made him feel wonderful. "How long have you had this pain?"

She removed the hanky. Karl noted with relief that her face wasn't swollen. "Since the first of February."

"That long? And you didn't tell me about it?" It could be any number of things. "Where does it hurt?"

She put both hands above her left breast. "Here!"

Karl frowned. "There?"

Jessica nodded mournfully. "Remember the day at the mall?" As if he could ever forget. "That's when it all began. I believe it's caused by loving someone and not being sure if that love is returned."

A variety of expressions flitted across Karl's face. Carefully he set down the tiny mirror he'd picked up, moved back the mechanical drill arm and touched the button that would return her chair to the upright position.

"If this is your idea of a joke, Jessica . . ." he said stiffly as pain lashed his insides.

She caught his arm. "Karl, look at me. Does it look as if I'm joking? I know you think I'm kind of pushy. I am, about certain things. But even I'm not that pushy that I'll chase a man who isn't interested in me. Look at me and tell me you don't care, and I'll leave right away and never bother you again."

Karl looked at her and sighed. "Life isn't that easy, Jessica."

"Who says it is?" Jessica retorted. "My mother always said every one is given a blank canvas when they're born.

The picture the paint on it is up to them. When we're young, others paint pictures for us, but the wonderful thing about the canvas is, each one has the ability to paint over the old pictures. As we grow, we have to bear that in mind. There is no limit to the changes we can make or the help we can ask to make our canvas beautiful. All it takes is strength of purpose.''

Karl stayed silent.

"You told me once beauty doesn't come out of a bottle," Jessica swept on, afraid to stop, to let thought take over. "Well, neither does happiness. It's a state of mind, an attitude, a strength one cultivates. No one controls your outlook but you. A strong person changes things—a weak one prefers to blame his shortcomings on others. You're not weak, Karl. If you'd only use your strength to help yourself."

As usual she was close to tears. Silence pooled around her, and as she calmed down, Jessica realized she never should have come. The shame of a personal refusal was going to compound her suffering. She stared at her hands as the tears ran unheeded down her face. A few seconds, and she would find the strength to stand up and leave. Right at this moment she was drained.

The silence stretched on and on.

Karl rose to his feet, crossed his arms across his chest, cleared his throat.

"About that pain you're having..." he began conversationally.

Jessica looked up, not bothering to hide the tears on her face.

"It's a chronic condition." Karl reached down and brushed her tears away. "You just have to live with it for the rest of your life."

"Oh?" Slowly hope filtered through, encouraged by the gleam in his eyes. "Is there anything you can prescribe that would help?" The words came out with the greatest difficulty.

"Marriage," he said thoughtfully, "marriage...to me."

"Oh, Karl!" Laughter and tears competed as she jumped up, wrapped her arms around him and laid her head against his chest. It felt so good just to be close to him again.

He lifted her face and stared into her eyes, searching for proof of her love. "Will you have me, Jessica?"

For answer she pulled his head down and pressed her lips to his. Karl reached behind him and switched the overhead lamp off. The stream of light from his office was enough to see by.

"Sweetheart, we have to talk," he said quite a while later.

Sitting in the patient's chair, he pulled her onto his lap and stole another kiss. "I'm still afraid I may hurt you sometimes."

"I may hurt you, too," retorted Jessica. "There aren't any rules we can follow for a perfect marriage. We have to make up our own as we go along. But love and communication help."

"I talked to a friend in Mexico this past week. Phil's a psychologist. He told me the conscious will is a formidable ally. I have to remember that only I'm in control of my life. Not my father, not the past." Karl snatched a kiss and said, "Will you keep me in line, Jessica?"

"We'll keep each other in line," she promised lightly, unwilling for him to see how deeply moved she was that he had bared his old wounds to a third person. The fact he'd done it all for her made her feel very humble.

"My father..."

"Your father was one man," said Jessica firmly. "You're another. My father's always been boss in our house. I know I can't be like my mother."

"You mean it won't be 'yes, dear and no, dear'?" Karl mocked wickedly. "And I just painted an obedient, submissive wife on my canvas."

"Well, it's a good thing you can paint right over that particular picture," Jessica retorted calmly, "because it simply will not do."

"What should I paint instead?" Karl teased.

"Paint love and trust and promises meant to be kept," Jessica said tenderly, framing his face in her small hands. "The rest we'll paint as we live it . . . one day at a time."

Three weeks later Karl and Jessica sat on the couch in his family room. She had spent a week with her family in Oakland, finalizing everything for the wedding. Karl had driven up Friday for the weekend. It was his second visit to her parents' home. A big wedding was planned in two weeks' time. Neither Karl nor Jessica could wait any longer. Fortunately, with everyone pitching in to help, they didn't have to.

Jessica thought of the noisy laughter, the comments that were typical when her family got together. All weekend there had been someone or other around, and Karl had been very quiet on the drive back to L.A.

"Did you find my family overpowering?" Maybe he was having qualms about the big wedding.

"Not really," Karl replied. "I was envious of all the friendship and the laughter, glad I'd be part of your family soon."

"Then why are you so quiet?" Jessica demanded.

"I'm just very nervous," Karl confessed.

"Nervous? Why?" asked Jessica, surprised. "They all liked you."

"I thought your parents might think I was too quiet and stuffy for their daughter."

From time to time she still caught a glimpse of the cracks of doubt. They were getting smaller, though. Jessica knew it would take time to convince Karl completely. She was content to let life and time paint that corner of their canvas.

She flung her arms around his neck. "As far as *I'm* concerned, you're perfect."

Tenderness softened Karl's face, and she saw the love shimmer in his eyes. "I don't know what I've ever done to deserve somcone as nice as you."

"Hush!" Jessica ordered, sealing his lips with hers.

Karl kissed her long and satisfyingly before raising his head to ask, "Did your mother ask if you were sure you wanted to go through with this?"

"No." Jessica nestled against her fiancé's strong shoulder. "She said there was a certain something about a woman in love. I have it, and she knows I'll be happy. She did ask if I'd told you I can't cook anything except eggs and chili."

"What did you say?"

"I said *you* could cook and I'd learn." Her laughter was muffled in the soft fabric of his shirt.

"Did you tell her you've decided to quit work?"

"Yes. I told her I've finally found the two things I really want to work at. The first is being a good wife and mother." Jessica watched Karl's face suffuse with tenderness. "The second is working for animal rights. They need champions. Humane shelters need more publicity, as well. There are so many people who can benefit from having a pet. Children, older people, those who are lonely. Look at the difference

Scrap has made in Mr. Lucas's life." Her face was lit from within as she talked of her dreams.

"You will save enough time for me, won't you?" Karl asked.

"Just like you will." Jessica's reply surprised him. "Mrs. Lucas and I have decided you're not going to work late anymore during the week and not at all on the weekends. She's letting all your patients know your new hours. If taking time for yourself worries you, she suggested getting a partner. She told me there's someone you helped through dental school who is very keen on working with you."

She was relieved when he smiled.

"I thought you were against dominance," Karl teased.

"I only said I was against *being* dominated," his wife-to-be said sweetly, tongue in cheek. "I never said I was against dominating."

"I'll have to get Reverend Barnes to include something about that in the vows then. Jessica Sylvia Hansen," Karl intoned in fair imitation of the minister he'd met yesterday, 'do you promise only to love and not to dominate this man?"

"I do," she said solemnly, her eyes alight with mischief. 'Except when it's for his own good, like working less, taking more time for himself and his family."

Karl groaned. "It would be just like you to say something like that at the wedding, in front of all the guests. I don't know why people call marriage 'settling down.' There's nothing about you that gives me the feeling we'll be doing any in the years to come."

Jessica smiled contentedly. "I don't think so, either, but you're going to love every minute of it."

Karl claimed one more kiss. "I believe that. Are you hungry? I'll fix us something to eat."

"Mom packed some cold turkey for us," Jessica told him. "Do you want me to make a salad to go with it?"

"I'll do it." He cupped her face in his large hands. "Jessica, are you really happy?"

She sensed the underlying concern in his voice, the sliver of the old fear. She smiled through the sudden moisture in her eyes. "Happier than I ever thought it was possible to be," she said seriously.

He hugged her before going into the kitchen and taking out the things for the salad from the refrigerator.

She watched him quietly for a while, reveling in the sight of him, painting her canvas with pictures of him holding a baby while a toddler scribbled with crayons and talked to a dog sitting nearby. She'd never realized when she'd volunteered for Project Valentine what a harvest of love she would reap for herself.

Going to Karl, Jessica wrapped her arms around him as he stood at the kitchen counter.

"I love you, Karl."

He turned to her, a glint in his eye, just as the doorbell rang. A huge frown creased his forehead. "I hope that's not Andy again. You are not to start discussing the wedding with her," he ordered. "The last time you did that, they were here till eleven and then you left when they did. Give Andy your mother's number and let her talk to your family all she wants. They'll all like that. I'll even pay her phone bill."

"That's a generous offer," Jessica teased.

"It's prompted by need, not generosity," Karl retorted. "My sister chooses the most awful times to drop in, and she always wants to talk for ages."

"She does?" Jessica said mock-innocently, remembering the session Andy had interrupted the last time. The memory made Jessica's smile even wider. "Let me get the door."

"If that's her," Karl called after Jessica on a note of inspiration, "say I've got the mumps and will be in quarantine till the day she sees me in church."

Jessica laughed. The ruby on her left hand winked back happily. She knew who was at the door. She opened the door and held a finger to her lips. The caller nodded understandingly and handed something over. Jessica blew him a kiss and shut the door.

"Who was it?" Karl asked when she went back into the kitchen a few minutes later.

"It's my engagement present for you."

"Engagement present?"

"Yes. You gave me this beautiful ring and so many other things. I wanted to get you something."

"You've already given me the most important thing in the world."

"Like what?" Jessica demanded.

"Love. Happiness. Faith in myself."

"I was motivated by pure self-interest." Jessica's grin didn't fool Karl. "This is something just for you."

"Where is it?" Karl looked at her empty hands.

"You have to close your eyes and come with me."

Smiling, Karl put his hand in hers and did as he was asked. Jessica led him into the hall and plopped a kiss on his warm lips.

"Open!" she commanded.

The dog sat patiently by the stairs, its leash looped through the rails. It looked at him and then away. Since Arthur, Karl had learned quite a bit about dogs. This one was a cross between a Labrador and a questionable breed. The large face looked very odd on the thin body. And very lovable.

He turned to Jessica and opened his arms to her.

"Do you like your present?" she asked.

He crushed her to his heart and kissed her. "Very much."

"Maggie likes you, too," she muttered into his chest. "She's been ill-treated by her past owners. When the neighbors reported it to the Humane Society, they went and picked her up. She was a mass of cuts and bruises. Time and love are all she needs."

Over Jessica's head, Karl smiled at the dog with the mournful, treacly eyes. With Jessica beside him, he knew he'd always have plenty of time and love to spare.

*   *   *   *   *

WRITTEN IN THE STARS

MAN FROM THE NORTH COUNTRY
by Laurie Paige

What does Cupid have planned for
the Aquarius man? Find out in February in
MAN FROM THE NORTH COUNTRY by
Laurie Paige—the second book in our
WRITTEN IN THE STARS series!

Brittney Chapel tried explaining the sensible
side of marriage to confirmed bachelor
Daniel Montclair, but the gorgeous grizzly bear
of a man from the north country wouldn't
respond to reason. What was a woman to do
with an unruly Aquarian? Tame him!

Spend the most romantic month of the year with
MAN FROM THE NORTH COUNTRY by
Laurie Paige in February. . . only from
Silhouette Romance.

MAN FROM THE NORTH COUNTRY by Laurie Paige is available in February at your favorite
retail outlet, or order your copy by sending your name, address, zip or postal code along with
a check or money order for $2.25 (please do not send cash), plus 75¢ postage and handling
($1.00 in Canada), payable to Silhouette Reader Service to:

In the U.S.
3010 Walden Ave.
P.O. Box 1396
Buffalo, NY 14269-1325

In Canada
P.O. Box 609
Fort Erie, Ontario
L2A 5X3

Canadian residents add applicable federal and provincial taxes.

FEBSTAR

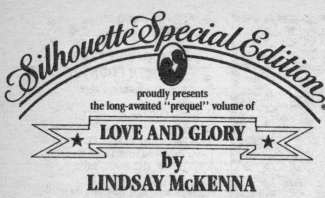

Silhouette Special Edition

proudly presents
the long-awaited "prequel" volume of

✦ LOVE AND GLORY ✦

by
LINDSAY McKENNA

Dawn of Valor

In the summer of '89, Silhouette Special Edition premiered three novels celebrating America's men and women in uniform: LOVE AND GLORY, by bestselling author Lindsay McKenna. Featured were the proud Trayherns, a military family as bold and patriotic as the American flag—three siblings valiantly battling the threat of dishonor, determined to triumph . . . in love and glory.

Now, discover the roots of the Trayhern brand of courage, as parents Chase and Rachel relive their earliest heartstopping experiences of survival and indomitable love, in

Dawn of Valor, Silhouette Special Edition #649

This month, experience the thrill of LOVE AND GLORY—from the very beginning!

Silhouette Books®

DV-1A

You'll flip . . . your pages won't!
Read paperbacks *hands-free* with

Book Mate · I

The perfect "mate" for all your romance paperbacks

Traveling • Vacationing • At Work • In Bed • Studying • Cooking • Eating

Perfect size for all standard paperbacks, this wonderful invention makes reading a pure pleasure! Ingenious design holds paperback books OPEN and FLAT so even wind can't ruffle pages— leaves your hands free to do other things. Reinforced, wipe-clean vinyl-covered holder flexes to let you turn pages without undoing the strap . . . supports paperbacks so well, they have the strength of hardcovers!

Pages turn WITHOUT opening the strap.

SEE-THROUGH STRAP

Reinforced back stays flat.

Built in bookmark

BOOK MARK

BACK COVER HOLDING STRIP

10" x 7¼", opened.
Snaps closed for easy carrying, too.

SILHOUETTE·INTIMATE·MOMENTS®

NORA ROBERTS
Night Shadow

People all over the city of Urbana were asking, Who was that masked man?

Assistant district attorney Deborah O'Roarke was the first to learn his secret identity . . . and her life would never be the same.

The stories of the lives and loves of the O'Roarke sisters began in January 1991 with NIGHT SHIFT, Silhouette Intimate Moments #365. And if you want to know more about Deborah and the man behind the mask, look for NIGHT SHADOW, Silhouette Intimate Moments #373, available in March at your favorite retail outlet.

NITE-1

BEGINNING IN FEBRUARY FROM

 **SILHOUETTE**

Western Lovers

An exciting new series by Elizabeth Lowell
Three fabulous love stories
Three sexy, tough, tantalizing heroes

In February, *Man of the Month* Tennessee Blackthorne in
OUTLAW
In March, Cash McQueen in *GRANITE MAN*
In April, Nevada Blackthorne in *WARRIOR*

WESTERN LOVERS—Men as tough and untamed as
the land they call home.

Only in *Silhouette Desire!*